THE MCTAVISH REGRESSIONS
ARABESQUE

THE MCTAVISH REGRESSIONS

ARABESQUE

LAYOVA AC
(ART COLLABORATIVE)

Copyright © 2020 Layova AC (Art Collaborative)

The moral right of the author has been asserted.

Apart from any fair dealing for the purposes of research or private study, or criticism or review, as permitted under the Copyright, Designs and Patents Act 1988, this publication may only be reproduced, stored or transmitted, in any form or by any means, with the prior permission in writing of the publishers, or in the case of reprographic reproduction in accordance with the terms of licences issued by the Copyright Licensing Agency. Enquiries concerning reproduction outside those terms should be sent to the publishers.

Matador
9 Priory Business Park,
Wistow Road, Kibworth Beauchamp,
Leicestershire. LE8 0RX
Tel: 0116 279 2299
Email: books@troubador.co.uk
Web: www.troubador.co.uk/matador
Twitter: @matadorbooks

ISBN 978 1838593 407

British Library Cataloguing in Publication Data.
A catalogue record for this book is available from the British Library.

Printed and bound by CPI Group (UK) Ltd, Croydon, CR0 4YY
Typeset in 10pt Sabon MT by Troubador Publishing Ltd, Leicester, UK

Matador is an imprint of Troubador Publishing Ltd

This is a work of fiction. Names, characters, businesses, places, events, locales, and incidents are either the products of the author's imagination or used in a fictitious manner. Any resemblance to actual persons, living or dead, or actual events is purely coincidental.

This book is not intended as a substitute for the medical advice of physicians. The reader should regularly consult a physician in matters relating to his/her physical or mental health and particularly with respect to any symptoms that may require diagnosis or medical attention.

The role played by Freud and Jung in this narrative is entirely fictional. The imagined Freud and Jung do, however, abide by the generally known facts of the real Freud's and Jung's life. The references, letters, dialogues and all the passages relating to psychoanalysis have no factual basis.

This literary series is for entertainment and educational purposes.

"And the day came when the risk to remain tight in a bud was more painful than the risk it took to blossom."

– Anaïs Nin

Dear Reader,

The heart shape left in my coffee grounds, as I take the last sip from my jumbo Corky Cup, reinforces the notion that my regression work has long since healed my own broken heart. Most mornings, I sit in calm reflection. My lives were well-lived but hard. I'm privileged and grateful that my journey has brought me here to you, patient reader, to give you some history on who I am and how I came to join you here today.

I spent my youth exploring questions that science cannot explain, and not much has changed since then. My methods have matured; that is, I no longer question the floating clouds overhead or the separation I feel from the Earth's core. I still, however, seek answers to the more mysterious, subjective, and relative questions: Who am I? Why am I here? What is a soul, and what does it have to do to reincarnate and evolve?

Seeking these answers led me to a lifetime of study in the behavioral sciences where I faced rigorous formal training in cognitive psychology, which, in turn, led me to the unconventional mental health approaches. Neurolinguistic programming (NLP), past-life regression, and Eastern medicine take precedence in my practice. You'll find me, on most days, in my comfortable office full of ancient memorabilia, taking people back to their souls' previous incarnations. I believe that past lives hold the secrets to this life's (dis)harmony.

Over my career, I've documented case studies with my faithful colleague, Professor Genevieve Buret, without whom I could not have carried out this work with such success, helping all who come to us. Vivi suggested we publish our body of work in the hope that it would bring *others to understand that their current life is an amalgamation of their previous lives lived on this beautiful planet. It is an honor to truly know this body/mind, as it acts as a carriage for our wholly unique souls, each on its painfully exquisite evolutionary path.*

We begin our presentation with Laura Tsvetkovsky, on whose regression case study, incidentally, was only the second time I met Vivi—a lifelong collaboration in the making!

It is with great hope that I wish our published work will improve your life. Enjoy Arabesque, dear reader, the first book in our heart-healing literary series, The McTavish Regressions.

Sincerely,

Wallace McTavish

1

Mano y Mano

"Thank you so much for taking the time to meet me, Dr. McTavish; I've waited a long time to meet you."

"Oh?"

"Yes. You wouldn't know this, but my thesis on criminal profiling from past lives had a section about you in it. When your assistant told me my appointment had been confirmed, I admit to a bit of a butterfly stomach."

"Well, butterflies are our business, after all. You must feel metaphorically comfortable then." Dr. Wallace McTavish knew all about her thesis and his being mentioned in it. The thought of criminal profiling through past-life events was a fascinating subject and he had a few questions for his interviewer himself.

The doctor's cool humor was matched by a black and white photo of him on his wall, probably taken not long ago, playing saxophone at what looked like The Lucky, a jazz club in Chelsea. Dr. Genevieve Buret recognized the stage and was duly impressed by his creative streak. She appreciated the doctor attempting to put her at ease and, as she looked around the bright study of his home, that ease was reinforced by his calm yet commanding demeanor. What struck her the most—not easily impressed—was the grace of the décor she noticed in the room. It had curios such as an antique whaling harpoon in the corner and Tibetan medicinal herb paintings in beautifully ornate gilded frames. These items stood opposing the library wall, juxtaposed with ultramodern furniture; it at once relaxed her and made her feel alert.

From the moment she arrived in Brooklyn, she couldn't stave off her anticipation at meeting Dr. McTavish. She'd probably had one too many coffees as she waited for the Uber that would take her to his curb, just a short distance from a cream-yellow and white porch. But an interesting wave of comfort happened as she closed the sedan door and stepped up the brick walkway. She couldn't tell if it was the scent of the roses or the rich variety of grass and ferns making up the front yard, but her nervousness had turned into simple curiosity. She was about to meet the man she hoped to one day call mentor. He was the kind of scholar you read about in history books, yet here he was alive and well, and plainly ready for her scrutiny. They called her "Vivi the Ferret" at school; if there were secrets, or anything untoward in a person's past, she would be able to find them. As a criminology scholar in her own right, Vivi had always felt a passion for metaphysics, yet, in reality, hated to suspect it having anything to do with her work. Still, some criminal mysteries couldn't be solved without it, and, now, she found herself here in this warm study, ready to further her investigations.

Not allowing her personal interests to take over, she returned her attention to smooth her pearl-gray pantsuit and present a steely professionalism. She turned on her smartphone recorder and opened the interview.

"I'd like to start with a few background questions. Dr. McTavish, how long have you been practicing past-life regression and what first got you interested in this fascinating subject?"

"I have been practicing past-life regression for about twenty-five years. In my teens, I became very interested in metaphysics. While going through a very tumultuous time, I experienced a sort of mini regression. It showed me the origin of some deeply held emotions and helped me to understand and then let go of them. Later, along the way, I had an epiphany that I should help others through this work."

His voice had a rhythmic, even undulating quality to it, and Vivi didn't want to admit that she fancied being hypnotized by it. She brought her next question after having to snap out of it a little, which surprised her.

"Past-life regression is a technique that uses hypnosis. Could you tell me a little more about your process? What are some things that separate your process from other practitioners?"

Before answering, Dr. McTavish took a long, slow breath. "Regression is reached through a normal relaxation induction, just like any other hypnosis: sitting in a comfortable recliner, feet up, eyes closed, soft music, and gentle suggestions to relax. This allows the memories to come into the mind. The client is able to talk with me and relate their experience as it happens. As a facilitator and guide through the process, my concern is to support the client in a safe place and at a safe distance as the memories are accessed. Before finishing, the client is directed to move into the highest levels of their mind. This, accompanied by the deepest relaxation, allows them to have an overview of their learnings, and then to release any part of that which has been creating limitations in the present. I do not know how other practitioners do it, but this technique has been successful for me."

"Why should people undergo past-life regression?"

"If a client has a fear or neurotic phobia that they can't relate to a specific experience, then it might point to a past-life event. Having relationship difficulties in this life; life patterns that keep repeating; an intense attraction or aversion to people, places, or time in history; sad, pervasive, and even obstructive feelings that can't be explained; a clear talent or gift that's very strong; and sometimes just curiosity are a few reasons clients come to me."

"What are some of the benefits?"

"Benefits include relief from negative feelings; explanation and resolution of certain feelings or patterns; release from fears, phobias, and fetishes; and acceptance, among others."

The room had taken on a very serious vibe, and Vivi was, so far, not disappointed in the answers she received. She decided to up the volume on the questions.

"What is the soul? There is the idea that past lives burden the soul with the accumulation of feelings from those past lives. Therefore, does undergoing past-life regression free the soul?"

"Ah, well, now, we're getting down to it." Without missing a beat, Dr. McTavish took great pleasure in talking about the soul. "Everyone has their own explanation of the soul, but my feeling is that it's the spark that makes us alive. It carries the memory of all past-life experiences, the personality and purpose or mission, into each incarnation. One might say that the karmic release during the process of past-life regression sets the soul 'free' from that burden."

"And what then is your opinion on critics of past-life regression who claim that the memories are not actual memories but social constructions?"

"Again, everyone is entitled to their own opinion. But I believe the emotion that arises during the regression is proof that it's coming from a very deep place within. While undergoing a regression, it's common to feel as if you're 'making this up' because it's such an unusual experience. My understanding is that dreams are about fifteen percent reality and eighty-five percent construct, and that regressions are the exact reverse, that is, eighty-five percent reality and fifteen percent construct. You are free to interpret this in your own way."

Dr. McTavish noticed her brow was furrowed by the intensity with which she was listening to him and kindly looked at the tea set. "Would you like a refill?"

There was no slowing down this mind, now almost obsessive in its attention toward the great man sitting in front of her. She felt a slight irritation that he'd interrupted her for something as insignificant as tea, but agreed nonetheless. As he poured, the space around them took a gentle spin into slow motion and she felt her shoulders and face relax. Unaware of how tense she'd been she felt slightly embarrassed but thankful for this moment to look around his office. The globe, the telescope, and some foreign book titles in his library, including Sanskrit, piqued her curiosity and she felt the need to study him through further research, though not in his presence. Vivi decided to ask only one last question, though she was not prepared for his response.

"Is there anything else you would like to say on past-life regression?"

"Most people think that a regression is experienced visually like a movie, but that only happens part of the time. It can also be experienced kinesthetically, as a thought, a knowing, a feeling, a smell, or just flashes, like still photographs. These are all valid. And even though much of the experience is interesting and enjoyable, parts of it can bring up some rather serious and traumatic experiences and intense emotions. There's no way to know ahead of time. Think of it as a valuable tool to help you understand your life circumstances and feelings that have no explanation.

"Sometimes what you dream about is a past-life memory fragment and not a Freudian symbol or metaphor or distortion. In waking life, perhaps you're traveling in a foreign country or city. You've never traveled there before but you know your way! We could call it déjà vu, but it's more than likely a past-life memory. Just being in the actual place evokes or stirs up your brain molecules, activating long-term memory to the degree that you might even smell the aromas of this past-life experience.

"So you have this déjà vu or meet someone who seems so familiar to you, as if you've known them forever, but you've just met them! Well, this kind of recognition is possibly a soul mate recognition and can also be a reflection of a past-life connection, so there are many other nonhypnotic ways of experiencing past lives.

"I think reading about cases can sometimes cause a resonance, or just identifying with other stories can remind you of otherwise stuck things, you know? Blocked imagery that your mind cannot let go of might just need a quick memory to release it. Then the brain is free to experience the current reality without the extra 'stowaways' on the ship. Memory stimulation and release happens and the healing can occur. We can experience these memory releases as starting a journey, during which we have the opportunity to go a little bit more directly into what makes up our inner worlds, why we act the way we do.

"Reading about cases is a fine way to familiarize yourself with the work. So let me show you the profiles of a few of my past lives, so you can get an idea about what we're looking into here. I've written them in somewhat of an artistic interpretation of the life I lived at the time. That is, I tried to document the events as the person I once was. I found a sense of solace in writing this way." He handed her a thick file filled with handwritten sheets of lined paper.

Shocked and called on the spot to read the documented past lives of Dr. McTavish put Vivi in an uncomfortable position for some reason. She felt entirely out of her depth, yet curiosity pulsed through her veins. What an odd sensation! He must have seen the stress in her eyes because he simply and calmly gave her a way out.

"Would you like to take them with you, to study at your leisure? Make copies perhaps?"

The fact that this person was handing over original copies of his handwritten past lives really threw her over the edge. But as a trained scholar, she simply did what all scholars did in this position: cleared her throat, blinked a few times, and nodded her assent formally.

"Thank you kindly for your time."

"If it's not too much to ask, would you return the files personally, please, I'm very interested in hearing how past-life regression meets the world of criminology. I plan to do some research myself, now that we've met, but your experience on the subject is invaluable, I'm sure."

At once she was flustered and honored by his interest. What had she opened up this can of worms for? She preferred living behind the scenes, but he was calling her out, and she decided to rise to the challenge.

"Yes, of course." Again with the scholarly demeanor. "I'll be in touch soon. I look forward to it. Goodbye, Dr. McTavish. This was a very informative meeting." *Ha! Informative? More like revelatory*, thought Vivi to herself as the doctor's assistant showed her out the large French doors.

"Goodbye." Dr. McTavish immediately turned to his computer and googled "criminology and past-life regression". To his pleasant surprise, there wasn't a drop of information.

1578
Newcastle, England

I remember myself as a stillborn, but that is not how recent history would tell it. There would be documented records of screaming and blood and tears, as all good births put forth on a Sunday in mid-winter. Apparently, the sun was not shining at 8 a.m. that morning, and all was red dolor and stink.

CRASH!

The Lord had me enter this world tied to a malcontent Catholic nun who, on the stench of my afterbirth, elegantly wept all of her sins out at once, like the sudden heat-exposed wither of chrysanthemums, and then she died. So, I suppose I just remember it wrongly, and it was she who tricked Death with an ol' switcheroo... her life for mine; clever for a sister, my mother.

Orphaned and at the hands of young, compassionate novitiates, I was taken to the cells over by the worn garden gates. There, they made me well, those lovers of God, who had been chosen for their aptitude in patience and quietude. They had not a clue, of course, as to the needs of a newborn, a sinner's boy, but assumed their duties thankfully, as gifts are wont to be received.

We all grew.

I remember now (slowly it's coming back to me more clearly) the first footings up into the rowan tree that shaded our habitude. She was a grand tree with fine layers of dust on her leaves and the scent of promises and laughter. I was often chided for running about barefooted and ill clothed, "You will catch a death by his tail and will not let go!" they would yell, not serious and knowing that I would soon be far out of range from their worries and fears. That tree was a mother to me, they all were, the nuns and the trees of St. Mary's of Kinn.

Oaks so tall that I even fell over once, in a trance from looking up too long at the canopy of the middle one down the lane. It grew sideways like an arbutus, as if the wind had made it pray all day long, since acorns. Oaks can sing, you know, right into your heart. When their choir was harmonizing within my own heart, I could see forever and a breath, as if I knew what forever was, and I did somehow, breathing with the next step up and then the next.

So you see how easily I have confused the memories, some synesthetic, some fable, all tragically beautiful, though especially on some Sundays at sunrise.

A young nun sits outside the cloister gathering sweet yams for the evening meal. In a moment of rest, she sees me sitting alone under the rowan at the far corner of the courtyard, especially glum for such a fine day. I didn't know it at the time, but she would become my lighthouse when my ship would crash back to the convent after each failed foster environment. I was a rotten soul, you see, never meaning to do harm but always managing to, criminally so. Humans are not designed to be boomerangs; I ended up hurting myself more deeply than I had started out.

I ran away from that sister, even though she was the only kind face I knew; it was too difficult to disappoint her time and again.

Barely attached to a scurvied body, they brought my dead, drug-addled brain back to the nunnery for burial. Young Sister Alice prepared my body for eternal peace with the same light she had used to greet me on all my other returns. She doused my winding sheet in lavender and rue, crossing herself nearly a thousand times before I was laid to rest that Sunday at sunset. Alice didn't shine quite so brightly thereafter.

1908
London, England

The summer Olympics brought our strong team from Bohemia; Maartje and I were on the figure skating team, coveting the gold but ending up with only memories, and me with a broken heart. She was the love of my life and she cruelly left me during the first week of competition. If you can believe it, she left me for a restoration artist, a British urák, just a sports fan with lots of money and a name. All over the camp, he'd *exaggerated the fortune of becoming her lover, and I found out, even though she tried to keep it from me.*

"What do you mean we can't continue; we committed to the stars our love!"

I couldn't understand the possibility of not touching the silk of her bones anymore. Her blonde mane, her tragic eyes, her whispers of contempt...

"It's not you," *she said, blinking rapidly so her heart would have less of a chance to be reasoned with.* "Can we talk outside?"

I shook my head several times no. "It's pouring rain outside, Maartje. Why can't we talk about this here?"

"I have to go practice," *she resigned with a shrug of her left shoulder, a tellingly cold gesture. She hated having to explain herself. Why couldn't people just accept things the way they were? Why go to such trouble to dissect confusion? The whole point is to avoid confusion. Clarity rules.*

"That's all there is to it. It's not you or me; it just is." *She figured a little philosophy would soothe me, but it didn't, and I released a frustrated shout.*

"You unsatisfied woman... do you understand the pressure that you put on me? To perform! I'm always guessing... I'm always fucking kowtowing, trying to find a way to reach you!"

"Trying to find a way to reach my pants, you mean. Yes, I understand, and I have to go now. I mean right now, really. As in: now."

She pointed to the ground with both hands for wide-eyed confirmation. Then she calmly got up from the bed where we'd spent the last week on the road together, it wasn't so easy back home, we had to hide our lesbian relationship. Now memory was wafting in the air to mix with the foul scent of betrayal. She put on new clothes—he must have bought them—until she was suddenly a new person standing in front of me. A traitor to her country and her sex.

"Bye."

I, the jilted of the two, was just watching her dress in shock and even a mild horror held her expression. I did not change my attitude of angrily placing arms akimbo, resting on the beautiful belt around my waist, which she had given me in our fourth year together. This was her last image of me. Oh—she most casually turned away and sneezed outside after closing the door on me for what would be the last time, never to see me again as long as I lived. Well, the process of elimination was satisfying enough for her, and I was left there, gutted by her spirit.

Hours would pass before I realized I had thought of nothing else but her. The weight and noise of our ended partnership would disappear, uninvited and hungry for resurrection. I took solace in my skating, the surrogate. Bereft, I had to return to the world where I am misidentified as a sexual criminal, never to find love again.

1952
Las Vegas, America

Mom is dancing with large feathers on her head and I'm watching with my wide, four-year-old eyes from the side of the stage. In the audience, pretty much everyone is wearing glasses. They all sit in groups of five or six, in these cool booths with leather studs, drinking amber liquid and tall clear liquid drinks. Mom's "The Main Attraction: Cherise Talour", and she sparkles just like a diamond.

We moved to Vegas just after we left Dad, not long ago. I didn't like him anyway because he would make Mom scared for days; I could tell by the shape of her mouth, and her eyes hardly blinked. She cooked and *stuff like normal, but she didn't really talk and looked at her watch and the back door a lot. I mainly played with Lego.*

Las Vegas was like one big Lego set, except with lights and fountains. Everybody was real happy all the time, like my mom's manager, Joey Debiasio; he talked real fast and wore rings on almost every finger. Mom's mouth was always smiling, and she blinked just fine. One day she was wearing a ring, too, a big shiny one with little feathers on the sides in gold. I bet it came from Uncle Joey, but I never found out.

Loreen was looking after me most of the time, and I was allowed to go to only the afternoon shows, when Mom performed as the star attraction. But then her star shows didn't start until way later, and I wasn't allowed to go anymore. Loreen and I would play Lego most of the time; well, she smoked a lot of cigarettes and drank that amber drink that smells weird, and I played Lego. I didn't notice, but there weren't other kids around in our condo complex. I learned how to swim, and the weather was always nice and sunny. I squinted a lot, looking up to the condo window to see if Mom was up and around. She and Joey slept in a lot.

One day, a real nice woman came to see us and gave me chocolate from her little red purse with snaps on it. It was a big bar of Hershey's. How did she know it was my favorite? I was so happy that day in front of the "damn cartoon box". That's what Joey called the TV. I ate my chocolate with Yosemite Sam, and Mom had a grown-up talk with the nice lady in the kitchen. When they had finished, Mom told me that the nice lady was going to take me on a trip to a big hotel for kids. I was so excited that I was going to meet other children I got my Lego ready right away.

Mom's mouth was different when she packed my bag, but I only glanced at her and kept packing, looking at her again. I wanted to make sure I had every last piece of Lego, even the little twosies. She hugged me hard and then lit a cigarette.

"Bye, squirt," Joey said to me from across the room, sitting with amber drinks on the table and not smiling at all. At least Mom was smiling with her weird mouth, and the nice lady had the same smile, kinda a half-smile, ya know?

"Bye." I held the nice lady's hand as we walked out into the hot day.

Turns out the kid's hotel was an orphanage, and I was the newest stray. 'Cept that didn't dawn on me until after about four days, when I'd asked the nice lady—whose name was Martha Day—when I would get to go back. It was a great place and all, but I was ready to go back to Mom.

"This is your new home, Jeffrey."

They had to chase after me, because as soon as I realized what was going on, I ran outside and headed straight for the highway. Kicking and screaming. That's how they brought me back each time I tried to get out, panting like a cheetah. I remember watching National Geographic with Mom about the cheetah. Fastest animal on four legs. I told Mom I could run faster than a cheetah and she laughed and said she bet I could. She bet I could.

Many years later, I wrote a poem for her:

Return

It is strange to be a corpse
the way you have left me lying here
gutted and torn by the crows that found me
in among the mallows
under the midday August sky

I will return as a whisper
in your silent moments

weaving a son's call on a wild loom
that crashes and splits its
tender wood just so you might listen

I know you will miss me
yet you were always missing something
so my absence will simply
blend into all the other
beautiful things you have thrown away

After Vivi read the last line of the poem, she found herself crying, but she didn't remember when she'd started to cry. In fact, she couldn't remember the last time she cried; it must have been as long ago as high school.

How much work Dr. McTavish must have done on himself to be the solid scholar and humanitarian that he was today, and after those tragic lives? He was a criminal in the first life; the case history certainly meets the profiling for his later years in that life. And now, he helped people get their lives on track. Having experienced such earthly hell would definitely provide the background knowledge to witness the same in others, and help them coax out their incarnations for the healing process to begin. Remarkable.

She wondered what her past lives had taught her. Maybe she had been a criminal also, which would explain why she could think like one today, and advise the police on how to track the more secretive, underground cases.

Over the next weeks, she looked forward to her meeting with Dr. McTavish, and she even entertained the idea of researching regression as a participant.

11

DREAMS R US

"What are we still doing here?" she sounded impatient yet respectful; the way Dr. Lorik scribbled in his notebook made her feel invisible. As if the data were magically going to fix her now. At least the pen, scratching its looped ink on and on, kept her from asking any more questions. They never answered her questions anyhow. So there she was in the clinic again, following the tip of the pen swirl around like a carnival merry-go-round, the horses rising and falling; her body beginning to sway.

"Laura... Laura, dear!" Her mother was forever interrupting her colorful daydreams, pretty much all the fun she had left in the adult life that was becoming clearer before her, nowhere to roll but toward the TV. She looked at the worried lines on her mother's brow and recoiled into the good-daughter routine. The guilt was unbearable. She was about to ask in a whisper if they could go, but the doctor interrupted.

"Sandra, I'm really liking the look of these results; let's discuss this further when I've had time to go over everything thoroughly. Can I call you tomorrow morning?

Laura thought to herself as she looked at her mother, *What a sycophant! Your smile will never be real until I can walk.*

She just wanted to wheel herself out of there as quick as she could. The rows of files surrounding her and the hush of the ugly mustard-yellow office carpet under her, well, hospitals gave her the creeps. In fact pretty much everything in her world gave her the creeps. Dreams were never Laura's problem; reality was what she could do without. She comfortably detached herself from her surroundings and the voices in the room sounded like they were in a drum somewhere far away. Her mother's voice, at a higher pitch, rattled questions off one after the other. Dr. Lorik set the baritone beat, bringing Laura visions of dust and dancing and bells and laughter. Even her spine felt alive for a brief moment, as she turned to see a woman staring at her from the hall. The scarf on her head was wrapped in a familiar way and Laura smelled olives out of nowhere, which made her frown. Back to reality, she saw the nurse coaxing the old woman away, the walker under her tense grip shifting to accommodate her shuffling feet. So suddenly familiar, her coal-black eyes shone toward Laura, with an odd similarly detached look in them. *Are we both dreaming?* Laura thought to herself,

I'll never get old and walk with a walker; I'll only roll the years away.

That bubble-popping, repetitive realization arrived. Their monthly departure from the doctor's office had started, as they'd now go through the motions of hopeful handshakes, see-you-soons, and the rest. She knew she'd watch So You Think You Can Dance when she got home, take enough meds to knock her senseless and sleep and dream, dream and sleep. This was what Laura looked forward to and was pretty much all the hope she had for her day, any day. Still, it could be worse. As an undercurrent, there always rested a deep sense of gratitude for the existing life she had. But it was her dancing that lifted her up to the "real" world—she let these thoughts wash her into the shadows and where the smooth sound of violins had her swaying in delight.

The hum of being an invalid was an undertone to every move; without her dancing, there would be no reason to live. The embarrassing sounds of the machine operated wheelchair lift, always too slow, as usual like sandpaper grating on the back of her neck, kept her looking straight ahead at the van console. How many times must she be forced to stare at the console buttons, the empty cellphone holder waiting for her mother to plug in and start up the positive thinking podcasts? And that rearview mirror air-freshener, dangling like a teardrop, occasionally changing shape from a tree to a lemon to a pineapple. She recalled the woman in the hallway and smelling olives, and how odd that moment was, and wondered if they made olive scented car fresheners. *I'll never change shape, why can't my legs move? They need to move!* Laura started her second round of harsh self-pity for the day. *I must stand at the bar; must have my teacher correct my arm and leg positions; need auditions, sex, love... Jesus, why am I stuck in this vaaaan?*

Finally, back at home, her private area was two identical rooms adjoined by a crude wall hacking that served as a doorway. A sledgehammer that her dad borrowed from the neighbor to give her some "wheeling room" had forged a way to make the two upper-floor bedrooms into one giant space. Her father thought she might learn to dance in the chair; it was a kind of useless gesture. Laura imagined a real dancer's life, with a mirrored wall and a bar of her own. Her imagination, however, slipped sometimes into dark corners, and today she found herself staring at her medication bottle, with a not-quite-formed ill intent creeping around in her mind. She imagined it guarding a portal onto a stage, being prepared for her opening night. Roses. Texts and Retweets. A world where rhythm and movement were king and queen, and Laura was the princess, receiving light from each leap and sweep of her arm.

The idea proved to hold her attention until she heard the kitchen stirring with plates and dinner preparation noises. She could just make out her mother prattling on to her dad about the day at the hospital, how great everything was and how she really felt this time they had a direction. Laura didn't hear her father say anything. Figures.

The heavy sighs were becoming longer and more frequent. Laura had pretty much resigned to letting her mother create the bullshit dreams she kept trying to sell her. More doctors or hospital trials. It's in a mother's nature to want the best for her child, but what she didn't understand was that the best had already happened. It existed. It wasn't outside of them, it wasn't something that her mother could find somewhere with a doctor's assistance. It was already alive and well in front of her, and that's what killed Laura the most, that her mother couldn't see her for who she was but yearned for a different daughter. But she was sitting there right in front of her the whole time! Are mothers always this blind or were these special circumstances just for Laura to assume the role of "can't-do" daughter, so that her mother would have a purpose.

She saw the way her brother and father looked at her mother, both of them wondering where the woman went who had once given them attention in equal measure. These last few years, where was the woman who'd been part of their lives? Maybe the fact that Laura had become a young adult brought Sandra back to her early twenties, when she wanted to be an anthropologist but married Henry, the amiable carpenter, instead. Perhaps she felt she was living vicariously through Laura, so she got a second chance to create the life she never had. But she was knocking on a proverbially locked door. Laura didn't have the tools to open it, so she just passively listened to her mother's repetitive and desperate knocking. She wheeled farther away with each knock, allowing the soothing rhythm to beat on the wood, giving their lives its own underscore…

It was ever clear that Laura's mind and heart were at one with the universe, and its pulse beat in her veins. The positions and pirouettes of her heart on a loop; her guts were the chorus, filtering the moves, all impressions went into the right places to sustain her God-given talent. Why was it taking so long? Where was the miracle? It's not even about fair or unfair, it's about *truth*. It's about the reality of dance irrigating her life. That's why she got up in the morning and why she went to bed satisfied at night, the polarity of light and dark forces could be clearly seen in any ballet!

I choose. I'm a superhero. A goddess of movement. I am in the womb of dance.

The floor looked dirty even though the cleaner had been there just the day before. The grooves between the wooden slats were dark and full of crumbs and Laura's throat tightened, when she realized she felt like falling down there in the cracks and never stopping. *I'll take two tonight, just tonight.*

She quickly grabbed the remote control and turned on a show, taking the second pill before settling in to other people's reality. Reality TV never had invalids on shows, did they? *No one would watch that crap.* She smoothed her dress, quickly brushed her hair, and put it up in a bun with the crisp, cinnamon-bun swirls of a prima ballerina assoluta.

I slope through a pretty fog; I dance the eternal dance I know to be like a feather. I am as simple and light as a fond angel dust train, like one of those antique pieces of furniture. No need for restoration. Its delicate presence and lofty Cherrywood lines in the room gives over of its noble grace to match my arabesque.

Laura turned up the volume to return her mind to the present and she knew she'd be finished with her pills by week's end. Maybe the doctor would prescribe something new, a fancy upgrade. Even though she called every doctor a prick, she understood they were trying to help her. She got it. She got that her mom was trying to help her, too, but there's so much sadness to wade through with her mother. She hated the thought that she was the burden for her mother's emotional hooks, jabbing under her arms as she lifted her into the car. As she lifted her around to the toilet. As she lifted her into the tub. At least Mom got a good physical workout with her for a daughter; she wasn't much more use than that.

Fumbling again for the TV remote control, Laura realized she'd popped one too many Xanax and barely had the sense to focus and settle on a dance documentary, *Argentine Tango*. Immediately she recognized the song *La Maza* by Mercedes Soza, and her upper body started to sway to the passionate music. The actual film was more than boring for an average viewer, but for the eyes of a depressed, would-be *milonguera* it allowed her to covet the moves of the older people. It looked like a South-American town square, and they were all doing some version of the beloved tango. None of them were professional, of course, but they could stand and smile and dance at least.

The next morning, Laura was up earlier than usual after a shameful night's sleep. She was jumpy on the inside, so decided to take another pill. Maybe she could still get some sleep, but it just made her woozy. So, for hours, she dreamed her dreams of gypsy kings and queens, dancing the night away with glee and passionate love for life. After dozing a bit, as she was staring down at her ballet slippers on the wall, she heard her mother call her for breakfast. She maneuvered her way to the banister mechanics to aid her downstairs. Another slow bridge to another banal family morning. The worst part of this endless up-and-down ritual was that she couldn't vary her movements like a normal person. She had to hook herself up onto the chairlift and have the family photos stare at her all the way down. From Grandpa to Aunty Phyllis at the bottom, or she started with her aunt and finished with her grandfather holding that damn fish he'd caught in Oregon. Her view, every single time. Lately, she'd starting closing her eyes as she slowly buzzed past the photos of her birthdays. From an early age, when she got her first "big-girl" wheelchair, her dad had custom made everything in the house to accommodate the bulk of her life companion. The dining-room table in the oldest photos could be seen set on blocks, so that Laura could wheel under it to blow out her candles. Then Henry built the family a proper table, and he made sure not to frame the sides so Laura could sit anywhere she liked. The end point of the lift would jolt her to awareness. This morning was no different, and, after the "eagle had landed", Laura wheeled her dopey form into the kitchen for breakfast.

She pointed to the ground with both hands for wide-eyed confirmation of her arrival, and then she calmly took her place at the table next to her brother, Danny.

"Hi."

Danny just looked at her purple leotard dress in shock and even with mild horror. His raised crumpled brow and roll of the eyes said it all. He didn't change his attitude of angrily placing his arms to rest on the table, which, incidentally, his parents kept telling him not to do. This was her image of him: Angry Arms.

"Did you jus' eye-roll me? Danny, get your smelly-lazy arms off the table." She turned away and sneezed and realized her words had been slightly slurred.

"You okay, hunny?" The ever-present doting mother asked insignificant questions again.

"Yeah, yeah. Just fine," she lied. Laura felt that relief of weightlessness, of being slightly beyond the reach of reality. No thoughts of others invaded her private mind and her heart remained remarkably silent. Hours would pass before she had a memory surge, and then that weight and noise of her gross life would reappear, uninvited and hungry for resurrection. She preferred to stay in the bonfire, with the surrogate… in the nomadic musical world where she was understood.

She dreamed on, imagining that the hovering smoke would soon fade and the embers from the party's fire the night before would do for a pot of coffee. She could smell the red pepper salad in front of her in real-time, but her vision, fueled by the great Dr. Lorik's prescription, was stronger. It took her some time to focus on having the food meet fork, meet mouth.

"Hey, Laura, I'm heading out to Dave's at eight, you want me to see if he's got that wireless speaker I told you about?" Now a young man, Danny tried less to be a definitive brother to Laura. There was the occasional recognition, though, if only so he wouldn't feel like the only shit-heel family member who didn't "support" his sister. She always bugged him about how his muscles didn't go with his red hair, calling him an oxy-*moron*. Why the hell should he support such a bitch?

"Naw. Not much point…"

"Danny, would you like some hash browns or *kanapki*?" The children's mother cradled the phone in her ear while she absentmindedly asked them all what they wanted but never fulfilled the answers. Their dad was helping serve the *kabanosy* eggs.

"Eggs?" I love eggs. He turned to Danny, "Eggs?"

"Yeah. And yes, Mom, to the hash browns, thank—"

"Really? Well, that's fantastic news," she turned from the phone and mouthed to Laura *we're in*. Another study, another trial. Sandra kept up with the conversation and ignored Danny's hash browns.

"So where do we go from here, when does it start? Next Monday? So soon?" Flipping the hash browns over, her voice had turned frantic, expectant, and frenetically hopeful.

Oh, Jesus, there's more disappointment in the close future. Laura couldn't help hanging her head low. Meds and guilt were not a good combo.

Danny snapped her to it with a squeeze on the shoulders and muttered, "Whatever, I'm outta here," and left his plate near full to meet Dave an hour early. He couldn't stand it at our house anymore; he and Dad barely even spoke anymore.

"Eggs?"

"Yeah."

That was about as much conversation as they'd had in a week.

The phone wailed again. Now Sandra was talking to her sister Phyllis, telling her all about the new trial; as usual, Laura was informed of her guinea pig status with this second-hand news. She turned to see her dad, glumly eating his bacon, staring out the window.

"Daddy? Fighting the good fight are you?" Laura tried to be kind and familiar, but her father had that look in his eye indicating he'd had enough of pretty much everything.

"Sandra, would you get off the phone please and come eat with your family? You already missed your youngest, as usual..." The sarcasm caught her off guard, and she told her sister she'd call back later.

Laura found herself staring at her father, whose eyes narrowed in contempt like hers did when she stared at her ballet shoes, at the pink that would never swirl under her feet. The creak of the refrigerator door brought Sandra to the table and she and Henry went at it, the eternal cursed conversation between them, with Laura in the middle.

"You have got to stop with your obsession of getting her to walk; we talked about this." Henry was more sad than angry now but still speaking as if his daughter weren't in the room. "Did you look Danny in the eye today? Did you smile at him even once? Wish him a good day?"

Sandra looked at Laura and immediately melted into a smile for her little girl, though not so little at twenty-four.

"*You* talk about it. I just listen… and I just want the best for Lor, Henry, what's wrong with that?"

"It's not enough anymore that you just want the best for her. There's no balance to our lives; it's all about Laura all the time, and it's as if we could leave the house and you wouldn't notice." Henry reached across the table to take his wife's hand, but she jumped up after Laura, who had left the kitchen. Henry was left to look around at the half-eaten food on the plates and empty seats of the kitchen table. *Where is my family?*

III

SWITCHING MINDS

The room was a womb, gently holding a life that assumed no active role in the world. It'd been a few days, and this morning was no different: Laura lay in bed, Still Life with the Curtains Drawn, feeling more like an erased pencil mark than a human. Her mother came in and out, quietly helping her to the bathroom, bathing her as usual, but, basically, leaving her in peace. She always appreciated that her mother didn't disturb her role as the depressed, young adult invalid. Her father on the other hand had another idea about living well.

When he brought her breakfast into her room that morning, he threw open the curtains and asked her what the hell she was doing with her life, that it was no way to behave for days on end, all bundled up in bed every day, day after day.

"I don't have anything to live for, Daddy, look at my legs; these are a *dancer's* legs, don't you get that?"

"I do get it, bunny. But the fact that your mother is trying to prove that you'll be able to or that it's an option is against everything I stand for—honey, believe me; I'm your biggest cheerleader."

"But you don't get it at all! It's *everything*, Dad. Dance. Is. Every. Thing. Not a wish. Not a dream. A r-e-a-l-i-t-y. It's everywhere I go! But no, access denied. I have to wheel myself. Who cares if there will never be any walking—only the dancing counts. The dancing!" She screamed a long lioness howl.

Henry tried to understand his daughter and was at a loss for what to do in this next second; she was obviously so fragile. "This is so hard for me to see you like this, Laura, I love you, your mother loves you, and we want to help you in any way we can."

"Oh really, Daddy? Mom's the only one trying." Her mother had just appeared at the door, wondering what the scream was all about. Henry motioned Sandra that they were fine, but she hovered around to make sure Laura wouldn't have one of her fits.

"Come and take a look at this picture on the front of your door," Henry said hopefully, "I want you to come and see what I see. I see a beautiful, bright mind, open to ideas, interested in the stars. Look at the size of that telescope next to you; you could barely use it then, and now it just sits in the corner of your room gathering dust. I want to know where that Laura went. I want to know where my little girl is. I miss her."

The words floated out of his mouth like a bad

cartoon and through the room, barely landing anywhere near Laura's common sense. He just didn't get it.

"That little girl is dancing in a parallel reality. That's where she is."

She was becoming increasingly depressed and it was time to talk to somebody about it. Her father left her plate of oranges and avocado on the dresser and he and her mother went downstairs. Her dad demanded that her mom look more deeply into the situation that was happening around them and effectively destroying their daughter. Laura could hear them downstairs.

"Empathy? Are you serious? What you're showing her is not empathy; you're just enabling this fantasy."

"I just want her to have hope. I cannot even begin to imagine the sorrow she must feel at not being able to live out her dreams, or even get a chance to attempt them, to have a chance at a halfway normal life!"

"Hope is one thing, but that's not what you're giving her. Laura is painfully aware of her reality and the only reason she goes on these trials is for you! So you'll have hope. Can't you see what's happening right in front of you? *She* pities *you*!"

Laura shook her head at how clearly her father knew her. She twisted her hands and tears filled her eyes again. Carefully lifting herself up a bit and rolling over in bed, she pulled out the pill bottle from underneath her pillow and slipped two of them into her mouth.

"All those appointments, Sandra; she doesn't want to go anymore!"

Laura closed her eyes and tightened her grasp on the bottle. *Here we go again, my trusted friends.*

Even though, that night, Laura had heard her mother finally agree to set up an appointment with a psychologist, when it finally came time to see her at the hospital, she couldn't help calling Dr. Lorik one more time to confirm it was the right way to go in Laura's therapy. Laura didn't seem to care one way or the other; it didn't make any difference to her where she was, so she agreed to go. Maybe this doctor would help her a little, and give her a new and more interesting cocktail of pills.

As it turned out, the acts of agreeing to go somewhere and actually doing it had quite a gulf between them, and Laura used every excuse in the book before admitting to the fact that she needed to talk this out with a professional. Her father finally changed her mind to get the help she now knew she needed. He told her the story of her birth and how excited he was to hold her in his arms, that he'd never known a love like that. Never knew he'd gladly do whatever it took for this tiny being to be happy, and could she just try a little harder to help him make those feelings a reality. Laura's heart hadn't felt anything for a long time. In fact, it wasn't until she heard those words from her dad that she realized how numb she had become. She was so moved by him that she nodded repeatedly and, in the moment, began to reach out for her chair. *They say love moves mountains, but I've never seen one move*, she thought.

The office had that we-want-you-to-feel-safe quality about it, with wide-open landscapes on the wall, pictures of pale peach skies with a solid house painted in the corner. Laura had been waiting about five minutes before the psychologist arrived, apologizing nonchalantly for her delay. But then they got right down to it.

"I'm Dr. Pasternak, Laura, pleased to meet you." When Laura didn't answer, she continued, "So your mother tells me that you haven't been feeling very well these days, what's going on?"

Laura stared at the desk in front of her, following the groove at the edges to meet the doctor's various papers and books, all holding "cases" just like hers. Being a case number turned her knuckles white as she clenched them, along with a couple handfuls of skirt. She had to play this just right to get the pills she needed. Trying not to grind her teeth too hard, she breathed deeply through her nose, exhaling her answer.

"I'm just tired—really tired."

The psychologist adjusted her titanium glasses, and Laura guessed this was textbook habit, to make the patient feel like they're being listened to. Aw, she seemed kind enough but a bit condescending, as she pushed a box of tissues toward Laura.

Dr. Pasternak asked, "Tired of what, Laura?"

God, why did they have to *do* that, use your name like it's the fucking Titanic or something?

Laura looked up at the psychologist, "It sucks

watching my dream die, and I'm so tired of living." She pointed to her wheelchair and smacked the armrests in a triumphant *duh* gesture. The psychologist started to scribble in one of her many notebooks, as doctors do. Laura was also suspicious of this fact; that they used that pad and pen as a buffer between them and their patients; why not just record the conversation, why pause it?

"And what's your dream, Laura?"

A gentle smile flashed across Laura's face before it faded, "I'm a dancer!"

The psychologist looked down and wrote another note, and she politely put down her pen and faced Laura, "And as a dancer, how does it make you feel that you can't actually dance?"

Laura narrowed her eyes at the psychologist. *Now she's thoroughly pissed over this psychology bullshit.* She pushed the tissue box back toward the doctor.

"Well, how do you think it makes me feel? It makes me mad." The tension in Laura's body gave way to a less defensive truth; she succumbed to being a clockwork case. "It makes me sad. Very sad." That was a nice touch.

Dr. Pasternak reached toward Laura's hand that flinched and retracted at the touch.

"I know you must feel sad, but we're here to discover a way to not let those emotions take over. We're going to try and find a way to stay positive."

Laura hunched her shoulders. "Look, I get it, alright? You're including yourself in this scenario like you have something to do with it, but it's only me that has to suffer here, so you can quit with the 'we' cheerleading, 'kay? And why don't you tell me what there is to be positive about anyway? How could you possibly understand the hole I face every day, the feelings of being lesser than everyone else? I'll never dance, and it crushes my mother, have you seen her? She looks like an old woman and she's only in her early fifties. What's positive about a woman who ignores every other responsibility except her crippled daughter? You'd think that she'd have better things to do by now, wouldn't you?"

"It's not your job to worry about your mother's wishes. Let's focus on you for now. You have a wonderful family. You're young. The whole world is just waiting at your fingertips for you to take it and try it on. Imagine all the amazing opportunities you have not limited by your disability; you have so much life you have yet to live."

Laura sat back in the chair and looked sideways at Dr. Pasternak. The choice of not having to take her mother's crises into consideration shifted her mood. And this made the room lift a bit; she noticed her breath was less labored, like a physical weight had been lifted from her chest. *What an interesting thought; my mother is not my responsibility. How sweet would that be?*

"You don't want to feel like this forever, do you?"

Laura shook her head. "No!" But inside she knew she wanted to numb any feeling, so she just needed to follow this shrink's lead, hopefully to oblivion.

The doctor was also noticeably more relaxed and sat back in her chair. She smiled and nodded emphatically, even knowingly, at Laura. "Would you agree that it is, in fact, 'we' who have some work to do? You're not in this alone."

Laura transferred herself to Dr. Pasternak's oversized blue chintz chair, a reasonable option to the more obvious couch that she expected. Gratefully, Laura noticed that her doctor didn't offer to help her; that's something that never happened. The lack of pity, or the fawning over her that she was used to, left a big question mark in the air for Laura: how was she going to fill that? It honestly felt great to simply start and finish something on her own initiative without anyone interrupting her with questions or concerns. The "can I help you?" was noticeably absent and, in her opinion, a cause for celebration.

Noticing the satisfied look on Laura's face, Dr. Pasternak said, "Any feelings you experience are normal. Many people go through myriad emotions, and it's important to address each one."

Laura rolled her eyes and then closed them, because she knew she was going to have to work this therapist. She felt something new stirring inside, some kind of yearning, but she quickly pushed it into the back of her thoughts.

"I just can't live like this, Dr. Pasternak..." she said and, after a long pause, admitted to herself and the doctor at the same time, "It feels like I'm drowning." Laura opened her eyes and stared at the therapist. Her eyes were dry and red. She just wanted to go home with a hard prescription refill.

"Well, Laura, first, you can call me Liz. And

second, you have the power to change your perspective. I know it doesn't seem like it just now, but once we set a few priorities and boundaries, you'll see you have more than just the power to do that."

Laura sunk into the chair and sighed. She acted all spaced out. The thought of having power was new to Laura, at least the kind of power that wasn't attached to using her disability as a weapon. She was aware that she could milk certain situations to her advantage, but she was sick of living like that. It was like eating chocolate cake every day; at some point, you just get bored of its decadence.

The therapist's voice began to head into Drum Land, and Laura made an intense effort to let the doctor think she'd gone off somewhere into her mind. It was no use. Her mind didn't need to give its permission for her to roll into the dreams that colored her life with rainbow shades. Today, she went to a blue pool, floating on an après dance high. Her body, full of endorphins, charged through the water like a mako shark. The energies that ran through her were not always about the actual act of dancing. Like, in this instance, it's after the dancing and she feels like a bionic woman, every muscle, each bone fulfilled with the magic that comes through her movements. Her legs whip through the water freely and the clear pool water rushes past like angels on her skin. The sky above her is a crisp cerulean cover, watching her in return. Now floating on her back she sees the overhanging bougainvillea and knows that there's a dry towel being held by her lover, waiting for her at the deep end. His feet dangle in the water as she approaches head first with a smile on her face, finally hoisting herself up into his arms and the warm plush caress of a cotton-linen blend—

"Laura… Laura? Are you with me?" Dr. Pasternak had been watching Laura during her daydream. Laura wasn't completely dissociated and didn't appear to exhibit any loss of consciousness. She noted that Laura freely moved between consciousness and a trance-like state of reverie. After two minutes of watching Laura, she decided to use the opportunity therapeutically. "How do you feel about telling me about what you just experienced? Was it a pleasant experience?"

Laura looked at the doctor sideways; her suspicions about her and any other doctor were not totally allayed, even though she felt really good with this person. She knew she would have to open up to Dr. Pasternak eventually, so she decided to do it today; why not? What could be the worst that would happen?

"Okay, Doct—uh, *Liz*. I'll tell you exactly what I experienced, but please don't tell my mom; she might think I'm getting worse."

"We're not concerned with your mother at all here, Laura. You're an adult and you have doctor–client privilege the same as any other client who comes in here. This is a safe place to explore anything you want. I feel that by looking into these periods of time, we can address some things that might help with the general therapy. Let me explain.

"As we go through the waking day, there will be times when the conscious mind is in the 'driver's seat', directing our behavior, because we need to think about some particular activity in order to do it. Then we might arrive at some task or activity that we've done a thousand times before, so there wouldn't be an immediate need to think about that. This is helpful to the conscious mind, so it can have a rest and take a backseat to the subconscious. Now we're on autopilot, taking us through the usual pattern of behavior; this state of mind is called 'trance.'"

"So I'm not crazy?"

"Certainly not! Ha, is that what you thought when you experience these dreams? That it was somehow abnormal?"

Laura inhaled deeply, and the air of her sigh was felt across the room; she was more relaxed now. "I get so nervous that I'm adding to my overloaded mind... I just have these compulsions to dance, and... well, you see I can't do that, so my mind takes over." She twisted the fringe on her dress a few times, and then, looking up at Dr. Pasternak she let the tears fall. "Yeah, I thought it was bonkers."

Dr. Pasternak gave Laura the time she needed to let the first wave of relief run its course through Laura's mind and body before she addressed what she thought to be her courageous patient.

"Right. This understanding often confuses people at first, because most think trance is something much more exotic than what you experienced just a moment ago. Most people think you need to have a hypnotist present, but in reality, trance is a normal state of mind in which we often reside to some degree, and we certainly don't need a hypnotist to get us in or out of it. When there's no need for your conscious mind and the subconscious directs your actions, you have dropped into trance. In fact, we're so accustomed to veering in and out of trance, we scarcely notice whether we're in trance or not. Acts like driving or operating any familiar tool, like a hairbrush for example, become habitual behavior. That is, your subconscious controls the act to the degree that you can do it without thinking consciously about it. Do you understand?"

"Well, I don't drive a car, though I'd be so afraid to because what if I trance when I'm in the middle of the road?"

"I find it very unlikely that that would happen. You might not realize it, but your mind would never endanger you; it really does need your permission to 'check out', and I think you might have developed this skill as a coping mechanism."

"You think it's a skill? Woah. Like, all this time, I've thought I was so messed up; now, you're telling me it's a good thing? That's so confusing." Laura shook a little, for effect.

"Trances like you experience are not remotely dangerous, and it's actually safer because the subconscious can easily handle several things at the same time, which the conscious mind finds almost impossible. Trance states are both normal and scarcely noticeable; even deep trances are common experiences, and this is what you're experiencing, Laura. Daydreaming is a trance state. If we go very deep into a daydream, we say we're 'miles away'. Active visualization about sunbathing can be very relaxing and even warm the body!"

"But I don't feel like I want to have these dreams; they just happen, and they feel so good, like the universe is finally paying attention…" Laura broke off into an Oscar-worthy self-pitying silence. She still didn't understand why, when all she ever wanted was to dance, that life brought her the opposite. *Can't we just deaden the pain already?*

"Believe me; the universe brought you exactly what you need, Laura. Thinking is a mental effort, so if you can avoid it that saves effort, right? Your brain is being energy-efficient. You drop into a sort of cruise control mode to experience the reality you choose. What you're experiencing is a deeper trance state than most. What I'd really like is for you to let me know what you're trancing about, would you agree to that?"

Laura thought to herself, *Here we go; there's no turning back now.* "I have these visions of me living a dancer's life. I'm either actually dancing or I'm before dancing or I'm after dancing. And it's wonderful, Doctor… I understand that during these trances the universe wants me to accomplish these movements, these…" she searched for the word, "events that happen. They're so real! So I oblige. For me, it's a far happier reality than the one I live in here." She motioned to the bright room and stared for a moment at the library; the colors of the book titles were so elegant. She thought maybe Dr. Pasternak chose her books for their design, and also noticed she had removed all the outer jackets of them, just like she did at home! "I need it. I need to go there."

"Well, Laura, these trance fantasies are quite normal, especially when you get a chance to live a life that you feel is far better than the one you've been given. But the whole point of our work together here today is to get you to understand that this life you're living is also full and rich and has every possibility in it. If you're physically challenged, then perhaps you could write about dance or draw—"

"NO, doctor! I'm a dancer! You don't understand, this is nonnegotiable." Laura amplified the reaction and she found herself actually suddenly very worked up, so she heavily set her chin against her collarbone. Now staring down at the oriental soumak carpet, she wondered why the hell someone would spend so much time just for the shape of a bird. *I need a magic carpet.*

Dr. Pasternak started to bring the session to a close. "I hear you. You need to dance. It's all about perspective and focus and…" Dr. Pasternak witnessed Laura's newly arising trance state and monitored Laura more closely this time.

The room shifts, and Laura no longer recognizes Dr. Pasternak's voice. She stays almost catatonic as the room becomes a clinic, with two nurses next to her; there's another pool and a male doctor stands behind her, holding her in the water. Past therapy sessions whizz by; she just needs to escape the doctor for a while. Scenes abruptly switch, now to a casual dining room. A tall and bejeweled woman sits at the ornate table draped in crimson velvet; she's reading tarot cards and Laura watches, immediately recognizing the *Zigeunerin* spread, fixating on each card as it appears. The red jewels on the woman's earrings begin to swing as she speaks the cards' messages:

"I counsel you to have patience."

There is no conversation. Laura is mute, simply listening to the chimes that the woman holds in her hand, shaking them as she continues the reading.

"Your mother may interfere in your relationships, whether she means to or not. Figure out where your boundaries lie with this, and let her know, so you can stay in touch with the beautiful part of her; she is simply one of the best people in your life.

"You will meet a wise, open, positive, adventurous masculine energy. You're likely to have an abundance of energy, which you're inclined to misuse; go in a positive direction."

Laura's memory suddenly shifts to a windowless room and she can see the incense holders; smoke billowing out of their starry windows, filling the air with a thick coat of reverence. A couple of sadhus sit in meditation with bright *tilaka* marks on their foreheads and large berries around their necks and wrists. She feels like she needs to say goodbye to the fortune teller and thank her for being so honest... She feels like she needs honesty more than anything.

Instantaneously, she's remembering the open countryside. Soft warm winds pass through her hair; she sees a horse stable in front of her, and the therapist walks up closely next to Laura with a magnificent horse. She's about to go for a "trust" ride when an office with a library appears.

Laura resumed consciousness and felt herself sitting in the chair. She asked in a timid and sleepy tone, "Was I gone long?" She noticed her muscles were extremely tense and hard as rock, but she just gazed out the window, lingering over her memory lane of therapeutic experiences.

Dr. Pasternak cleared her throat and said with a smile, "Not at all, I timed it at four minutes. I think we'll put a pin in it here for today, Laura. Good?"

Laura shook her head out a bit as she returned to reality, readjusting her eyes to focus on the psychiatrist. "I'm sorry, I—"

"Quite alright." Dr. Pasternak stood up and walked to her desk. She picked up her pad and pen, writing slowly as she kept a gentle eye on Laura. "I'm making an adjustment to your medication, adding something called Tegretol and Diazepam. Tegretol is for seizures, and I believe it'll help to make the trances less traumatic when they come on and subside, while still allowing you to experience them. Diazepam will help with the depression; it's an opiate, so you must make sure to only take the prescribed dose."

Bingo. Laura hoisted herself up in the chair, feeling a bit dozy but otherwise elated. She was happy to have

Dr. Pasternak look after her mind, which she now felt wasn't her enemy, and gets a nice treat soon.

Settling into her wheelchair, she noticed how much had happened in one little hour, how things have changed. She knew because her stomach tremors were gone and that was the first time she ever realized she even had stomach tremors. Laura accepted the new prescription, which, now a stronger blot-out-the-world ticket to ride, gave her the heavy joy she'd need for the next phase in life. She really appreciated the fact that Dr. Pasternak tried to convince her there was nothing wrong. That was the best part of this show. "Thanks."

Laura hated taking the bus, especially at this time of day when everyone was coming home from work and had to "politely wait for the crippled girl" to get situated in the handicapped section of the bus. *Just let them appreciate their leg muscles, the idiots*, Laura thought to herself, the first of the new meds kicking in, *how beautiful their legs move, the body is a finer machine than my wheelchair.*

As she waited for the 409 at the stop not far from Dr. Pasternak's building, she saw a figure in the distance that she was sure she'd seen before. The walker and the speed. The look in the old woman's eye. Her approaching prompted a flash of recognition, and, once again, the smell of tangy olives hung in the air. But Laura couldn't place where she'd seen those eyes before, now smiling directly at her and shining like tiny black stars.

"Hello, Missy, mind if I sit?" Laura watched the top of her scarf as the woman got comfortable, which took a decidedly long amount of time. She wasn't fussy, just slower than anyone Laura had ever seen. But she moved gracefully, Laura noticed, like she didn't waste a drop of energy in getting from here to there.

Finally still on her bus stop bench, she looked at Laura sideways and smiled widely, showing a perfect set of dentures, so incongruent with the rest of her shriveled form.

"Nice teeth." Laura was surprised she'd said something so familiar to the woman. She felt like the pills perhaps had removed a filter. She quickly corrected herself, "I don't mean to be so personal, it's just that your teeth look like a new car—uh, I mean, they look nice."

"Thank you, child, they are, in fact, new, and they'll be doing some fine chewing in about two hours' time." She made a little *chop-chop* sound, as she mock ate, looking rather like a wild wolf!

Laura giggled. "I'll bet."

Without missing a beat, the woman said she thought that she might have been a wild animal in one of her previous lives, what with the way she could devour a steak. Laura thought how uncanny it was that she remarked on that just after she had thought about her being a wolf.

"I love me some T-bones…" again with the *chop-chop*, and then she spoke rather seriously to Laura, "I wonder what you were in your previous life?"

Laura could honestly not come up with one thought after that; it was as if her brain had gone numb and stood in the middle of her skull without a care in the world. Luckily for her, it functioned well enough to make out the bus number. She took off her chair brakes and inched out toward the curb a bit. "This is my bus."

The old woman reached out and patted Laura so gently on her hand that she felt as if she'd been blessed. "Take care, sweetheart," she said and didn't stop looking at her until the bus pulled out from its hospital stop. Leaving the old lady seemed profound somehow, with her walker and colorful headscarf zooming out of view, her sitting peacefully on the bench. Laura found herself wondering which bus the woman had been waiting for, as there wouldn't be another one passing by there for some time. Her hand seemed to tingle inside from the woman's touch and soon the bus engine drowned out her every thought, and she dozed for most of the way home.

Laundry day, Laura's mother called out to her from the basement, "Laaaaura? What's this business card in your hoodie pocket?"

"Wha—?" Laura was looming over her upstairs window, looking at how far a drop it was to the lawn below. She dismissed the possibility of an "accident" and her mother's voice shocked her out of her fantasy. "What's that?"

"This business card here, for a Dr. McTavish, PhD, CH." Sandra was at her door now, exaggeratedly enunciating the title on the card in her inquiring voice, suddenly so near, she gave Laura a second start.

"Jeez, Mom, sneak up on a person, why don't ya." Laura wheeled over to where she was standing with a mother-accusing-daughter look in her eye, and those damned pursed lips. "This was in *my* hoodie; you sure?"

"Do I look like I'm unsure? Now you tell me this minute, what the hell is a CH? And what kind of doctor has feathers floating all over his business card? Some quack for sure. Where did you get this?"

"I—uh…" Laura took the card thoughtfully, "I honestly don't know. But let's call him, maybe it's a referral from Dr. Pasternak. Oh, by the way, she gave me a new set of puppy uppers for my 'depression'." Laura couldn't help doing air quotes, the calling card waving right along with her.

"Oh? She didn't say anything to me."

"That's because I'm an adult, Mom, fully capable of taking care of my own mental health, even though you and Dad think I have so little left of it."

"Well that's not true and you know it. Now, how about a nice T-bone steak for dinner?" *Deflecting emotion with uncomfortable meal suggestions, typical.*

After writing her mother off as a kind of irritating loser, the old woman from the bus stop immediately came to Laura's mind, and she couldn't help but give a long, loud wolf howl. Laughing, she looked at the business card and started to google the particulars on her phone: D-r-.-M-c-T—

"What has gotten into you? I'm going to call Dr. Pasternak for a consult; just to be sure we're on the right track."

"Whatever, Mom, you go ahead. Meanwhile, I've found our mystery doctor; he's a hypnotherapist." Laura's voice trailed off dreamily as she remembered the old woman talking about reincarnation. Could she have slipped her the card? What a sneak! She resolutely decided on a hunch to call Dr. McTavish and set the soonest possible appointment. Something about this felt absolutely correct, even fated, a feeling Laura hadn't had in a long while or maybe ever. Her mother's voice rang and rotated in the background like a siren. She was complaining about something or other, still going, as she wheeled away to take a closer look at the track record of Dr. McTavish, Certified Hypnotherapist, "CH." With her back to her mother, Laura absentmindedly popped another pill, as she scrolled through the doctor's impressive online presence. *Huh.*

IV

FREUD MEETS JUNG

If Vivi thought she'd been thrilled to have met Dr. McTavish the first time, this next meeting had her in an absolute professional tizzy. Would he answer all her questions? Would it sound like she was interviewing him or grilling him under an investigation light? She laughed at the thought and hoped he would be interested in her collaborative ideas. She could profile her perpetrators, with his permission to put them under hypnosis, to get into their psyches and see where and how they'd lived before now, to give her a glimpse into why they'd committed their current crimes.

There was very little formal academic study in this field of combining criminology and past-life regression. Surely, her colleagues would think her mad, but she knew there was something to it and had to explore her leads. This nagging these last few weeks had kept her up at night more than she'd like to admit, and Vivi's preparations for her meeting with the doctor today were comprehensive and only the beginning. This was what she'd hoped to share with her father, an eminent scholar in his own right, but he never really had time for Vivi, and when he did, it was never enough.

She was sitting in the same thick leather chair as her last visit, impatiently waiting for Dr. McTavish to arrive. She'd already put the past-life material on his large oak desk, grateful that he had trusted her with the notes. Remarkable. When he arrived, she could barely contain her excitement and retain her aura of professionalism. She had many questions, and by the time they were halfway through their first cup of tea, he'd answered many of them. He now approached the reasoning behind his personal interest in hypnotherapy and how it had clearly been his professional path from the beginning.

"You'll have noticed the past lives I gave you to review, among others, revolve around the subject of loss, betrayal, and abandonment, and, many times, this happened to me when I was a young male. As a youth in my current life, I had great difficulty trusting anyone, including my parents and especially my mother. I used to think she made up words, just for effect, you know? And later I'd find in the dictionary that she'd been correct, *spatula* for example; as a young child, I thought she was lying to me.

"So that's the reason I became so curious about other peoples' lives and minds. It's also why I went into the behavioral sciences because I wanted to know if there were others who lived with suspicion, as I did.

"Along the way in early graduate school, I'd studied Jung's later works and his reincarnation experiments; I came across the material of Dr. Ian Stevenson. His findings quite simply changed my life, and steered me toward what you see as my practice today."

"Yes, I've heard of his working with people who have current life afflictions or birthmarks that correlate to previous life memories of violent deaths."

"That's exactly right. In fact, I have a young woman coming here today for her first therapy session. The pathology is really quite interesting. Perhaps you'd like to watch a recording of the consultation? I'd value your opinion."

"Certainly." Cool as a cucumber on the outside, shaking with excitement like *tzatziki* on the inside, Vivi couldn't have been more thrilled, and chose to direct the conversation to Dr. McTavish's questions. "You mentioned your interest in how hypnotherapy could work in tandem with criminology?"

Dr. McTavish took a long drink of his now cold tea. "Yes, indeed. Let's get another cuppa first."

After he'd arranged for his assistant, Gilda, to bring more tea, Dr. McTavish launched into his theory. He thought perhaps current life recidivists, not one-time criminal offenders, could be regressed to various lives to find and release their deviant behaviors. By confronting their phobic and other survival scenarios, and therefore releasing their current life tendency to present the same or opposing behavior, they might avoid institutionalization and have a chance at a normalized life not behind bars. Of course, much research would need to be done. And they'd need viable quantification methods for further study, but he believed it could be done and he proposed another meeting where they would both bring their thoughts for a more formal study environment.

"Looks like we have some serious architecture to commit to!" Vivi exclaimed, not hiding her jubilance about the idea. "Think of the possibilities for crime reduction and better quality of living; I'm glad you feel so strongly about it. One thing, though; I feel I should have a regression myself, so I can work from a place of knowledge. Is that something you'd be willing to do?"

"Agreed. In fact I'd go as far as to say that I think a personal regression session is a prerequisite to our work. We could find another regressionist, should you feel more comfortable in an objective environment."

"No, I trust you implicitly, Dr. McTavish."

"Very well, we can set that up for another time. Meanwhile, if there wasn't anything else, I need to prepare for my client, Laura Tsvetkovsky. She was born without the use of her legs and has an almost pathological fixation on dancing. After consulting with her attending psychologist, Dr. Pasternak, we're going to start her regression series today. I'll send you the tape later for your review."

"Looking forward to it." Vivi stood up with vigor and she was clearly impressed with Dr. McTavish's respect for her work. "Goodbye."

As Dr. McTavish said his farewells to Dr. Buret, he also smiled inwardly, for he knew they'd both just turned the corner into the groundbreaking research that would occupy their practice for many years to come. He mused: *Criminal Minds: Reincarnated How Many Times?*

V

THE DANCER

"Would you like to work directly on a past-life experience for yourself? I have some music that we're going to play so we can start that, if you like."

"Yeah okay, I guess so. What kind of music?"

"Just new-agey groovy stuff, like, electronic soothing whale music, except without the whales."

Laura liked this old man and his sense of humor. The way he moved reminded her of someone, but she couldn't place it; a professor she knew from TV, maybe? "Okay."

"We'll find a good level for the music and this will go on for about three minutes or so. Getting comfortable is important, and finding a position you can fully drop your body into is perfect. Does your chair recline slightly? Maybe a pillow would help?" Dr. McTavish brought Laura a long, oddly shaped pillow;

actually, it looked like a giant lilac lady finger. It fit perfectly on the back of the chair and Laura could let her head recline.

On his way back to the desk, the doctor closed the venetian blinds, the thick wooden slats slowly closing out the light in the room.

"I'm so glad you decided to come and visit us. Most people don't understand regressive therapy. Some even think it might seem a little strange at first."

Laura coughed out a laugh. "Nothing seems strange to me anymore. I've pretty much done every kind of therapy imaginable."

"And none of them worked?" Dr. McTavish smiled knowingly.

Laura frowned and shook her head with an angry emphasis. "Not in the least."

"Let me explain a little about regressive therapy. We use hypnosis to allow you to explore your inner world."

Laura shifted in her chair.

"We're not here to change you or give you a solution. We're here to help you find your own answers."

Laura sat back in her chair. She pointed toward Dr. McTavish's impressive library and said, "You like to read. I need to dance. These are just the facts. Have you ever heard of Maya Plisetskaya? Bolshoi. *The Dying Swan*. Arms folded, on tiptoe, she dreamily and slowly circles the stage. By even, gliding motions of the hands, returning to the background from where she came out, she seems to strive toward the horizon, as though in just a moment more, she will fly—exploring the confines of space with her soul." Laura reeled her upper body left and right, performing the movements. "The tension gradually fades and she sinks to earth, arms waving faintly, as if the swan is in pain. Then faltering with irregular steps toward the edge of the stage—leg bones quiver like the strings of a harp—by one swift forward-gliding motion of the right foot to earth, she sinks on the left knee—the aerial creature struggling against earthly bonds; and there, transfixed by pain, she dies."

"That sounds very moving, Laura."

Laura got a kick out of that, and broke character, back into stubborn patient mode. "Meh. Some critic wrote it about her. It's what I was meant to do. So what, in this regression business, the answers are spoken to me by some mystical person inside my head?" Laura chuckled and kept the smile on her face.

"Well, I told you we aren't like other therapies. Sometimes, the world inside of you is full of memories from your past or your past lives."

Laura leaned forward and arched her brows. "Oh really?" She nodded, keeping a hardcore sarcastic expression planted on her face.

Dr. McTavish kept his even tone. "And sometimes, it's your internal world that you explore. But either way, you'll have to find the answers there yourself."

"Okay. So how does this work?"

"My assistant and I will start hypnosis and put you into a trance. You'll be aware of what's going on at all times."

Laura nodded her head, *okay, a trance, that's something I can relate to*.

"You mean play pretend?"

"The longer you're in the world of your mind, the more it will feel like reality. You won't even need to pretend."

"So, it won't hurt or anything, right?" She took over the wheels through the back door.

"Not at all. Some emotional issues might arise, but you won't feel any physical pain."

The egg-white room had a matching chaise longue in the center and an elegant chandelier hanging over it that reminded Laura of *The Dying Swan*, so elegant in its form. A light played in the background, and even though Laura wanted to have a weird *Phantom of the Opera* type vibe about all this, it was literally one of the coolest places she'd ever been. The doctor's assistant helped her onto the chaise longue and she caught Laura's eyes with a questioning "that okay?" look. Laura agreed and adjusted herself to comfortably look up at the chandelier, as it swayed. Dr. McTavish walked over to the wall and dimmed the lights. The music faded in softly.

"Are you ready?"

Laura twisted her hands together. Her body was tense. "Mm… yes."

"Relax. The process is dependent on you releasing your tension and falling into your subconscious.'

"Okay. I'm trying."

"Listen to my voice. Follow it as it leads you down a path, far from this room."

Laura focused on the doctor's voice as she laid her hands in her lap. She stretched her fingers out and balled them into fists several times to relax.

"Watch as the light sways in front of your eyes. Back and forth. Back and forth." Laura's eyes followed the chandelier. Her hands relaxed. "Close your eyes and slide into your mind as the world around you fades away." Laura's eyes closed. "Open your mind… quiet your thoughts… We're ready to begin. It's very safe here and you can open your eyes at any time. If you feel stressed or uncomfortable in any way, feel free to open your eyes at any time. Or go back to a beautiful beach that I'll describe, or you can also just float above any scene or experience and detach from it.

"So you're watching from a distance; whatever comes into your mind and into your immediate awareness is just fine. Are you with me so far?"

The music was playing at this point and Laura smiled to herself because it was exactly whale music without the whales. She nodded to the doctor, and he continued.

"Everything that arises is perfectly fine, no need to analyze or critique, just experience it. Whatever you experience is fine, even if it seems unusual or silly; just experience it.

"Focus on your breathing and use your imagination, whatever imagery finds its way into your mind is fine. So, breathe out stress; breathe in beautiful energy that relaxes your whole body. Relax deeper and deeper and relax all of your muscles: your face and your jaw; so soft, so relaxed, letting go of all tightness and tension in these muscles."

Dr. McTavish's voice suddenly sounded so familiar. She felt maybe she'd heard a lecture from him before she dropped out of philosophy, but she remembered that now wasn't the time for analyzing. Laura quickly let the association go and listened to his dreamy tone.

"And the muscles of your neck and shoulders relaxing completely; just take this weight off, relax your shoulders, let go. Go deeper and now deeply relaxed, let my voice carry you. Deeper and now even more deeply relaxed, let any background noises or thoughts or distractions just deepen your level even more, as they fade away…

"Relax your arms, your upper and lower back. You go deeper and deeper into a beautiful state of serenity and calm. Peace is healthy for you, the healthiest feeling for your body and mind. To relax, to let go of stress and tension, to find this peacefulness, this is always there for you just below the surface."

Dr. McTavish continued with his soft speech through the entire body until Laura's whole body was melded into the chaise longue. She didn't know where she stopped and the structure began; she felt at one with the whole room.

"There's a beautiful healing light above your head. It is a spiritual light connected to the light above and around you. Let this beautiful light come into your body through the top of your head, illuminating your brain and spinal cord and healing the body's organs and flowing down from above to below like a beautiful wave of light, touching every cell of your body, filling it with peace and love and healing.

"The light fills your heart; imagine you are wrapped in a beautiful cocoon of light. It wraps around you and heals your skin protecting you completely and deepening your level of relaxation. Your mind is no longer limited by the usual barriers of space or time, so deep that you can remember every experience you have ever had whether in this body or in any other body.

"You are always loved; you are never alone and you can never be harmed, not at this level, going deeper and deeper. Imagine now that you're walking on a beautiful beach, a wonderful spiritual beach next to a vast ocean, and the area is filled with sand and flowers and plants and other beautiful things. It is a beach garden, a sanctuary for you: a haven, a place of perfect peace, perfect safety.

"Bliss. Joy. Love. You find a place to rest in this beautiful beach garden. Let's begin going backwards in time, at first a little bit and then more and more…"

Laura followed Dr. McTavish onward, listening and responding to every step along this beautiful light-filled beach garden. She followed his voice as it led her back further in time and she found herself in a childhood memory in her neighbor's kitchen. There was the scent of freshly baked lasagna and the sound of the hockey game on the TV. It wasn't difficult to move on from there back in time even further until she was standing outside in a large field, next to a water tower.

Dr. McTavish's voice guided Laura on… "What do you become aware of? What do you look like? Is it visual or just feeling or hearing or smelling or tasting…

"You are still with the memory; it is trying to tell you something to remind you of something or someone. When I count from one to three you go through your birth with no pain at all. One: being born, no pain; two, three: you're out, you're born and there's a beautiful door. Your past life is on the other side of this beautiful door. I count down from five and as I reach one, you will reach that past-life scene. Five: the door begins to open; beautiful light pulls you to the other side of this door. Four: you move through the light closer and closer to the scene. Three: joining the scene you find yourself in a body, look down at your feet. Two: you become aware of other people; observe how they are dressed or what they are doing and if you get close enough to another person observing their face or their eyes. One: your energy is there, you can move forwards or backwards through time—"

VI

CATALAN 1592

Laura's eyes open and she blinks wildly as she looks around a small room, with only a single candle's light filtering out the darkness. After focusing a while, she can make out lengths of soft and shiny fabrics draped across and hanging down from the ceiling over the mattress she's lying on. She reaches out gingerly to touch them; feeling that they're real, and she scans her arm in amazement as it moves in front of her. She rolls over, and her legs stretch out. The suddenness of her legs moving stops her immediately. The excitement wells up inside her chest at the realization that she can actually move her legs, and the pleasure she takes in the next several movements cannot be compared to any other she has felt; any other movement than her dancing, that is. She sits up and looks down at her feet.

Woah! She touches her legs, and her skin is amazing! She deigns to bend her knees, and yes, this is happening; slowly she rises to a standing position and lets the exhilaration of the moment run through her. *I—I can walk?* She takes a couple of steps forward, stretches her arms out and giddily walks toward the door. As she is passing a mirror she stops short: looking back at her is a teenager with a black mass of curly hair and large dark eyes. Laura's eyes widen, and her mouth drops open. *Is this me?* She approaches the mirror as if meeting an alien and caresses her face with her hand while simultaneously touching the mirror for proof. She licks her lips and tucks her hair behind her ears; then shakes her head wildly and lets out a tiny scream of joy as she jumps into the air for the first time in her life. Defying gravity is freedom. Her hair bounces around her face as she dances maniacally in the mirror. Hallelujah, what a miracle—a crash comes from outside. She stops and turns, abruptly stopping her celebration. Laura steps forward and opens the door.

Laura stumbles out of the covered wooden wagon, astonished as she drinks in the world before her eyes. A couple of wagons with men, women, and children are scattered throughout the camp. Dust, levity, cheer, she happily skips down the steps and stops again to further scan her new digs.

A very old woman sits under a tree, smoking a small pipe and peeling something or maybe just whittling some wood or a root; she looks to be about a hundred. Children whiz by laughing in bright clothes and bare feet. All the women are busy with one task or another. It's a cacophony of sounds and action. Laura sees outdoor kitchens with steam and smoke billowing from each one; big black pots hovering above fires, tended to by gnarled hands. Dark scarves cover the heads of these women, stirring their soups and stews for the day. What aromas!

Gamblers, palm readers, and story tellers, it looks like a movie set. Laura keeps pinching herself to make sure this is actually happening.

A large beautiful woman with healthy skin is taking down laundry from the line next to the wagon, which Laura now notices is round like a tunnel. This woman turns with the basket full of clothes and saunters over to Laura, her hair and eyes are soft and wild at the same time. Laura's heart swells with love as the woman approaches.

"Finally, my little swan wakes from her deep slumber."

Gillie hands the basket to Laura, who buckles from the weight but recovers quickly. Her mother gives her a little look as if to say, *what was that all about?* but also recovers quickly.

"Now, it's time to work before Papa sees you. Huh?"

Laura nods her head briefly and realizes that her eyes are still wide with surprise. She clears her throat to assume a natural manner as a few children run up to her.

A young boy with blackened teeth and shaggy hair grabs Laura's skirt and flies in for a hug; she just about drops the laundry again.

The boy asks loud and clear, "Aishe, you going to dance with us? Laura looks down into the boy's eyes, and he too looks wild and soft. Gillie walks over and grabs the boy's shoulder.

Laura asks herself, *WTF is going on… so weird, dance*?

"Not now, Bo. Aishe is busy with clothes and other chores. Work first, play later." Gillie winks at the boy, turns him by the shoulders, and pushes him away. Bo runs with all the other children as Gillie calls after him, "What did Mama say, *el meu nen*, Bo?"

"Work first, play later!" Hahaha, the children run off to their games and dancing. Laura watches them, and her eyes tear a little—what emotional people, like her!

The rest of the day has Laura confused but enthusiastic about her new environment. She spends the night out under the stars in a hammock, by her mother's suggestion. Apparently, she'd folded the laundry "like a camel" and didn't know where to do the dinner dishes, so Gillie thought her daughter needed alone time to regroup. Amazed in her hammock, she falls asleep to the sound of fires crackling and owls hooting suggestions for her dreams to come. She would, however, have no dreams to remember, sleeping like a rock through the night and waking only at the chilly dawn.

Laura wraps a beautifully embroidered wool scarf around her and walks through the Cigano camp. She stares at a group of men as they lift a rolled-up rug over their shoulders. The older man with a full gray beard grunts, as he walks bowlegged with the other younger men, hauling the rug onto a cart. Laura, so fixated on the scene, stumbles into a woman, who actually hisses at her and shakes some herbs in her face. She recognizes her from the day before as the woman who was reading palms. Surprised, Laura flinches backward a couple of steps, only to bump into a large, heavy-breathing man, as weathered and wild as the others. What she didn't expect was the bear hug that he locked her in to steady her fall. The bear hug turned into a regular hug as he looked tenderly into her face with the big grin of a mountain man.

"Aye, my little swan," his baritone laughter kept the surprises coming, "Have you lost your eyes?"

Laura pushes away from the man, but soon her heart educates her that this is her father, Luca, coming back from a lumber trip. "I'm so sorry, Papa!"

"That's no way to treat your Papa." Luca opens his arms for another hug, and Laura steps in for the warmth and safety he provides. He lifts her off the ground in a swirl and Laura is at once embarrassed and full of joy, her eyes wide with admiration for this strong man. She relaxes her body, and Luca sets her down, both of them smiling with love.

"And why do you have such a silly grin on your face, my swan?" Laura looks up at Luca and is still in culture shock; she knows he must see it.

She laughs. "No reason."

Luca grabs the sides of Laura's head like a doll and plants a kiss on her forehead. "Mwah!" She steps back from Luca and looks up at him with a look that only a wild daughter could give.

Laura turns to join the group but pauses on the way, her head spinning a bit, like channels flipping back and forth on a fifties' TV: her reality switches suddenly to her present life and her dad, Henry, comes into focus. Laura sits in her wheelchair. She's six years old and it's dark and quiet outside. Henry holds her shoulders and guides her chair toward a telescope. Her dad smiles at her, as he points up into the night sky. Her mom comes up to the roof with a plate of smores, and Laura can taste the chocolate and marshmallow hanging from her mouth. Henry tousles Laura's hair and gives her a big kiss on the forehead. Everything is warm and cozy and still; love fills her heart as Henry wraps his arm around Sandra's shoulder, and they watch their sweet daughter look through the telescope. The stars go on forever.

"I'm glad my little swan is happy. Now scoot, before your Mama sees I'm being too soft." Luca releases his daughter and walks in the other direction. Disoriented, Laura snaps back to the camp and wonders how the wires crossed. Not wanting to return to any wheelchair, she spins on her heel and starts running toward her mother and the other women, working under the willow trees. Laura, glowing from the love of her *two* fathers, now fully switches channels again as if by remote, she skips toward the camp women. She smiles and waltzes toward Gillie, full of gratitude for the use of her gorgeous legs; what a world… Her mother and a couple of other women working by the river gather gray willow switches for basket weaving. Laura passes an older woman, squatting near a basket, peeling grapefruit. Laura bends down and grabs a couple of pieces from the basket, and the woman swats away Laura's hand. Giggling, Laura winks at her and dances off to her mother.

"Mama, anymore chores? Or can I go dance now?"

Gillie looks up at Laura, laughing heartily. "What am I going to do with you, my little swan?" Gillie turns to the other ladies. She playfully whips at her with a willow rod. "Always the dancing with her."

Laura skips over to Gillie, grabs a rod of her own and twirls her mother arm-in-arm as they whip their willow rods like fencers. All the women laugh and clap as the family duo have a lark. Then back to work.

"So, can I go dance?"

"Go on, before I change my mind."

Laura squeals and claps her hands in thanks.

"Don't forget you are going to town with Papa later."

"I won't! I won't!"

She could hear her friends long before she saw them, kicking up dust near the stream. They're drinking and dancing and clapping, and the guitars and laughter fill her soul.

The musicians wave Laura over, and she rushes to join the fun. They continue to sing their passionate songs as the rest of the group gets four rhythms of clapping going. The stomping heels match the tempo, and the dancing goes on for hours, until Laura remembers she must accompany her father to town.

Waving her hands with dancing gestures, she says goodbye to her friends and runs to the camp stables to meet Luca, already waiting for her in a horse drawn wagon. Out of breath and very happy, Laura hops up onto the bench and her father whups the reins for the horses to giddy up, "*Arrii!*"

After a beautiful ride in the countryside, Laura still doesn't know exactly where she is or what language she's speaking, but from her history studies, she assumes somewhere in southern Europe. They enter a small town with a couple of buildings and drive right through to the other side, where they arrive at a big church. Luca had been telling Laura funny stories about his recent lumber trip, but now he turns serious and looks sideways at Laura.

"So, my little Aishe, you will soon be leaving Papa."

She looks up at Luca. "Leaving you?"

Luca laughs deep from his belly. "Tonight, we announce your husband to be."

"Why? I mean, I want to stay with you and Mama. I want to be free to dance and do as I please."

"It is tradition, my swan." Luca drives the wagon into the church courtyard. "I'm sure you won't be too disappointed with my choice." Luca parks the wagon in front of the giant wooden doors of the church. He jumps down and whistles. The massive church doors swing open and an old, gray-haired monk greets them with a smile. Laura stands and jumps down from the wagon.

"Greetings! Have you brought *la gallinas* that I asked for? They're going to make a fine soup, Luca."

Luca nods his head low at the monk and walks to the back of the wagon. "Yes, brother. Five fresh *gallinas* as ordered, good and fat."

The monk smiles and turns his attention to Laura. "How are you doing, Aishe?"

Laura steps forward and begins to respond, but her father interrupts. "Ah, she is fine. Soon to be engaged."

The monk turns to Luca and before he takes the hens from him, crosses his heart and the two old friends grab each other's arms in a formal shake of celebration.

"Well! Congratulations to you all."

"Thank you, Padre! We are very pleased with the match. Tonight, we make the announcement."

Laura stares at the two men and waves of questions flow through her, though she knows somehow, the situation is necessary and that she has little power over her family's plans. The men grab the hens and carry them into the church, and there's one left so Laura helps to bring in the last bird, passing it to the monk as he and her father return to the wagon.

"Thank you, Aishe." The monk unties a bag of coins from his cincture and hands it to Luca. "We will see you next week! Oh, and Aishe, may God bless your union." Laura nods her head in thanks and, as Luca says his goodbyes to the padre, Laura gets the wagon ready for departure, first saying hello to the horses and giving them each an apple that she found on a nearby tree.

As she and her father leave the church, Laura tells Luca that she thinks the padre is a nice man.

"Indeed!" Luca and the monk have been doing business for many years, over which time they have become good friends. "But not all Spaniards are as nice as him."

Laura knows instinctively what her father is talking about: the Romani people have always been a marginalized group, not adhering to the Christian faith that spread so aggressively through the land for these last hundreds of years. Enough stories have been told around the campfire to educate the youth that they must always keep their guard up around the *payos*, the non-Roma. To them, the *Gitano* are not real Spaniards, and the Church doesn't like those who live a nomadic free-roaming life with the Earth; those who do not worship their God.

A group of townsfolk join the Romani crowd who have made a circle around a tall intense figure, standing still in its center. Hats, peppered with *escudos*, mark the four corners of his dance floor. A hush waves through the onlookers as the first strings of the guitar vibrate then quickly stop. Again... and stop. Marko, a young commanding dancer from a neighboring village, begins to silently and slowly clap his hands in front of his eyes, staring down at something far off so intently that the small audience look for themselves, but they soon realize the focus of the dancer must be coming from within. A group of large men begin to follow Marko's rhythm and loudly clap their various staccato *palmas* to lead the guitar and, finally, a slamming of feet begins the dance. ¡*Baile!* ¡*Ole!*

Luca and Laura have come to watch, magnetized by the howling and singing that has now joined the other musicians. Shouts from the crowd fly in the air, along with *escudos*, some hitting the hats but most of them missing, modestly adding to the dust flying up under Marko's feet, as his body leaps and sways to the wild rhythm. Laura stares at Marko and doesn't notice that her mouth has dropped open and her body has begun to sway to the beat, locked in a gaze with Marko's eyes. She thinks the makeshift floorboard under his boots might crack under his power.

"What do you find so fascinating, *el meu elegante cisne?*" Laura keeps staring. Luca clears his throat. "My swan? Hmn?"

"Sorry, Papa! It's his dance. It reminds me of something, but I'm not sure what."

"Well, are you going to stand there all day? Join them! I'm sure you could teach that boy a step or two." Laura looks at Luca and smiles. She hops through the circle, pushing past the crowd on her way to the center. Marko spins on one foot. He plants his other foot out in front of him, like a horse, and faces Laura. This is an unspoken language, an invitation. Marko smiles and stares down Laura this time, while he slowly begins to dance again.

"Aishe, are you going to join me or not?" Laura smiles at Marko and steps into the circle. She begins to shadow his movements, and, soon, they are dancing the rhythms from their ancestors, lost in a timeless conversation.

"¡*Baile!* Give us a fire." Laura claps and stamps her feet rhythmically. The audience begins to mimic her beat. She shuffles her feet to the sound of clapping *palmas*, completely in her element. The audience focuses on her and Marko stops and steps aside to watch her as well. She picks up momentum. She arches her back. Her arms rise. When her arms reach the highest point, she rolls her wrists, elegant claws, snapping to the fire she has kindled in her heart. She continues to sway her arms and wrists to the beat. Marko's heels bang their way over to her in a Catalan *golpe*, and he playfully snatches her by the waist, drawing her into him to dance. Laura's cheeks redden.

Now that they can speak without shouting, even though the crowd is going crazy with delight at this point: *ai, ai, aiee!!!* Marko asks her with genuine praise, "And where did *that* come from, *benita*?"

"Ha! I have no idea. I just felt it." Marko grabs her hand and spins her out of his arms. The open smiles between them heighten the theatrics. They continue to dance.

Luca realizes he's going to have to pick up the weekly supplies himself, as he watches his lovely daughter lose herself in the dance she so passionately loves. He backhands a stranger's shoulder next to him and says with bittersweet resolution, "*Ai, el meu*, Aishe, *el meu* daughter is a woman now. What's a father to do?"

Laura and a couple of young Romani sit at a small table. Talking and laughing among themselves, they see military men ride into the village on magnificent horses, with shining steel standing out on their uniforms and saddles. They do not speak to anyone. One dismounts and walks to a tree in the center of the camp. There, he hammers a letter to the tree. Looking around with a menacing smirk, he rejoins his troop and rides noisily out of the camp. Laura stands up and walks across the courtyard to read the sign.

By the order of
La Tribunal Del Santo Oficio De La Inquisicion

King Ferdinand II of Aragon and Queen Isabella of Castile, all gypsies are to disperse in no more than 30 days.

No two gypsies are to be seen together or they will suffer the consequences of the law.

Laura gasps and lifts her hand to her mouth. Gillie walks up to the tree and, noticing her daughter is distraught, takes Laura's arm as she begins to read. A couple of other Romani crowd around to see and they all begin to express their shock and questions.

Laura turns to Gillie. "Mama, what does this mean? Will we go to prison?"

Gillie coughs out a haughty laugh. She grabs Laura's hand. "No, my dear. This is the Spaniards' way of trying to tame us. First, they told us we must settle down. Now, they tell us to go." But Laura grabs Gillie's hand with both of her hands, tears in her eyes.

"Don't worry, Aishe!" She smooths her daughter's hair, whispering with passion, "They can't change who we are. We will always be a proud people and culture. You cannot tame the heart that has Romani magic inside. Never!"

A pig rotates on the spit of a gigantic bonfire. Romani crowd around the fire, drinking and dancing to the music. Laura twirls around with a couple of young ladies, their skirts flying wide like a bat's wings stretched out in the night. Laura's curls bounce in her face as she catches Marko's eye. He's sitting by the fireside with a couple of young men, storytelling, drinking mugs of ale, and laughing as brothers do. Laura stops twirling and cannot believe the blush that comes to her cheeks just from eye contact with Marko! He grins back at her.

Just then, Gillie comes up next to Laura and grabs her arm. "Come with me, my little swan." Gillie leads Laura into the covered wagon. Inside, a lamp glows orange. Under her mirror on the wall, Gillie grabs a little box off the tiny silver shelf and hands it to Laura. "When I was a young girl, my mama gave me this the night my engagement was announced."

Laura opens the box and stares in wonder as she lifts up a leather necklace with a rose crystal dangling at the bottom, catching the light like her mother's kind eyes. Laura caresses the gem as if it were a precious diamond, looking up at her mother, eyes brimming with tears.

"It's beautiful, Mama! I love you so much. But I—"

"What is it, *cisne*? Tell Mama," asks Gillie with raised eyebrows.

"I just don't know about this. How can I leave the two people I love the most for someone I don't really know?"

Gillie lifts her hands up and takes Laura's jaw into them, firm and loving. "You're not leaving us. You're just finding a new dance partner. You two will learn to sway together to the music of life." Gillie walks behind Laura and ties the necklace around her neck. "Do not fear. Your father loves you; I love you. We just want to see you happy. Let's get out there and find out who your match will be." Laura holds onto the crystal as she follows her mother back out to the festivities. She only then realizes it's her engagement party.

A proud father sweeps his hand toward his lovely daughter as she steps down from the caravan. He's standing right at the center of the party and waves Laura and Gillie over to him.

"Now, for my special news." He bows and grabs Gillie by the waist, drawing her close with a big kiss. "My beautiful wife Gillie and I are proud to announce that our little swan will soon be a bride herself!" Shouts of joy come from the community, most of the elders already knew, of course. Luca ushers Laura into the center of the group.

Another older couple step forward and usher with a wave a young man to the opposite side of the center, Marko stands and walks toward Laura. Again, she blushes!

"When Marko and his family first approached me to ask for my Aishe's hand, I asked Marko, 'What do you think of my daughter?' and looked at him closely for the truth. He said, 'She is my partner in every way,' and that was after drinking *one* ale." He waits with one finger in the air. "So, I said to myself, I said, 'Luca? You lucky father-in-law, imagine how in love he'll be after two ales or more!' Aha! Aha, haha!" Luca laughs, his baritone ringing out into the cool air. The crowd joins in with giggles and laughter, clapping and shouting to the love birds.

Then a serious tone falls on the group, as one would feel when walking into a sacred forest.

"When you get married, you become responsible for your wife and your future children. The burden is often hard." Luca grabs a mug of ale and solemnly lifts it up above his head. "But whatever you do, don't spend your time arguing, it will put gray in your beard and shorten your life." Taking a ceremonious and giant swig of his ale, he starts to laugh, foam still on his mustache. "Once, Gillie gave me the silent treatment for an entire week. A week! At the end of that, I declared, 'Hey, we're getting along pretty great lately!'" The crowd begins to roar with laughter, and the musicians respond with a lively tune. "So tonight," Luca shouts with great pride, "we drink, dance, and celebrate the future of this beautiful couple. Marko and Aishe, may your love last for eternity!"

The camp is quiet. Only a few folks are up and about; after such a late night of festivities, it's possible they haven't even gone to bed.

Laura pops out of the wagon to greet her first day as a betrothed woman. She still stretches like a little girl, though, her arms way out to the side, mouth wide with a deep yawn. Luca comes up to her and pokes her in her belly.

"Tsk! Papa!"

Luca laughs with deep love for his child in his heart. "Today, my *chiquita* swan, you will be going on your first outing with your husband to be. I'm not sure if I am meant to be proud or worried."

Laura blushes, but recovers from her embarrassment as she realizes that this is simply how life is; she's a bride to be, and that's that. "It's not a big deal. We're just going to the village, to perform."

Marko surprises Laura by joining in on her explanation; she hadn't seen or heard him walk up behind them. "With Aishe's new moves, we're sure to line our pockets with silver." Laura jumps forward a little toward Marko, clearly excited about the prospect of dancing the day away with her beau. She lowers her head a tad and blushes.

Luca takes great joy in seeing he has chosen the right man for his daughter's future husband. Laughing, he says, "No big deal, huh?"

Laura stands tall, and she whips her skirt ¡*Ole!* She squints in playful reproach at Luca. "Shouldn't we be going, Marko?" Marko nods and gives Luca a big smile and a strong pat on the back.

"I'll take care of Aishe, Luca. She's a treasure."

"I'm counting on it, *hijo*!"

Marko walks toward the wagon. Laura smirks at Luca as she leaves to walk with her man. Giddy with excitement, she hops inside, sitting up front.

Luca remembers his catch of meat for delivery. "Ah! Marko! Do you mind dropping off some meat to the monk?" Luca walks to the wagon with the six colorful birds, hanging upside down, long resigned to their fate. Laura turns around in her seat as she watches Marko jump down from the driver's seat to retrieve the catch.

"Of course, Papa! No trouble at all, Luca." Marko loads the fowl onto the wagon back, covering them with a blanket. Luca is clearly impressed with the knowing way his soon-to-be son-in-law handles the work, and his daughter. *Ah! Life is good.*

"Stay safe, *nens*, my children…" Marko cracks the reins onto the horses and the wagon lurches toward its journey, the two love birds quite content in each other's company. Laura waves at Luca. "Don't worry, Papa, we'll be home soon."

Marko and Laura pull up to the familiar church where her friend, Brother Guillermo, tends to the garden, watering the bushes with wide buckets, almost too heavy for him to lift. Marko rushes to his aid.

A little surprised but very pleased at the act, the monk turns toward Laura and greets her warmly.

"*Buenos matin*, Aishe." The monk lets Marko continue and walks over to the wagon. Laura hops down from her seat and rushes toward the aging monk with a big smile and news of the birds.

"Morning, Padre! My father sent us with the *gallinas* for you."

"Bless you, *nens*. And who might that be?"

Popping up from the garden with a large pail of

water swooshing over the roses Marko says, "I am Marko, Aishe's husband to be."

Brother Guillermo puts out his arms toward Laura and Marko returns, drying his hands on his shirt before also embracing the monk's arms, in both a more formal greeting between them and a congratulatory shake of approval from Brother Guillermo.

"Well, congratulations are in order."

"Thank you! We are very happy," Marko says softly and looks at Laura with a sweet grin.

"*Bo. Bo*. Very good… would you bring the order inside for me, please?" Marko turns and walks back toward the wagon. Laura follows.

"Yes, Luca gave us six birds for you." Laura leans against the wagon as Marko grabs the hens and hands them to the monk, who hands over the leather pouch of *escudos*.

"Just in time. We are in need of extra meat. Guests have just arrived this morning. Please tell Luca I said thanks, they look like lovely birds, as always."

Laura steps forward and suggests to the monk that they stay for his guests. "Maybe your dinner companions might want a little entertainment?"

Marko turns toward Laura and clears his throat.

Laura looks at Marko and shrugs. "What? Who doesn't love a little dancing?"

"Er… I don't think they would make a good audience for you, Aishe. In fact, child, I suggest you not perform until after our guests leave the village."

Laura tilts her head sideways, confused by the monk's remarks.

Marko turns toward the monk and is quite serious. "We thank you for your suggestion, but we are Romani. This is who we are." An awkward moment hangs but quickly passes, and the good-natured feeling among the three returns as Marko and Laura hop back onto the wagon.

As the young couple wave their goodbyes, Laura turns to Marko and asks him what the monk meant by suggesting they shouldn't dance.

"Don't worry about it, Aishe; he's just an overly cautious man. He probably doesn't want too much dust blowing into his church, ha! We'll be fine, *meu amor*." Laura realizes that's the first time he's called her his love, and she's very pleased; all this is so new, but it feels right. She also feels that he's covering up some other reason that Brother Guillermo said what he did, but she knows she's safe with Marko. They start the horses toward the village square.

The monk raises his hand in a blessing, "*Déu us beneeixi*, God bless you."

"And to you, brother!" Marko smiles and nods to the monk. Laura grins and waves goodbye, watching the white roses as they disappear from view.

A crowd forms around Laura and Marko, who are staring each other down in the passion so accustomed to the wild dancing of the Romani. Marko rests on one knee, shouts and claps, "Fire!" Laura dances to the beat. She twists her arms and wrists and skirt, as she had done in the camp. The villagers begin to clap and stomp to Marko's beat, happily cheering Laura on as she dances.

Across the square, a soldier tosses a young man with a wounded head out of the tax collector's office. This makes quite a racket, and the dancing stops, with the confused crowd looking on. Laura stares at the tall young soldier, clearly an aggressive man, with his beard carved so perfectly around his face; he looks like an evil animal to her.

Stepping through the doorway to yell at the man he'd just thrown out, the soldier sees everyone looking at him, and this only feeds his power.

"How dare you come in here looking for a position unsuitable to your rank. The thought of it! A Marrano could never serve our sovereign king, who would never look at you let alone allow you to work for him."

The wounded man's sickly wife runs to his side. "Isaiah, are you okay?"

But he pushes her away as he tries to get up and shouts at the soldier, "I am just as much entitled to an honorable job as you are. My mother was a fine Spanish woman."

The soldier begins to giggle to himself as a few more guards and finely dressed Spaniards walk out of the office to join the commotion.

"Yes, but your father was a filthy Jew. You will forever have infected blood." At this, he spits on the man, still struggling to stand upright.

Isaiah's wife snaps back at the soldier, "How dare you? My husband is a decent man." The officer takes offense and easily grabs the woman by the arm and tosses her away to the side. She cowers at the soldier's strength.

"Shut up, *tu puta*. Talk to me like that again, and I'll teach you a lesson."

An elegantly dressed gentleman steps forward, known to the villagers as Juan Valdos. He very calmly and clearly addresses Isaiah, now standing, holding his wife in a feeble attempt to protect her.

"Sir, I am the Regional Magistrate. I was sent to ensure that this village follows the rules and guidelines set by our sovereign monarch and the church."

The whole crowd, including Laura and Marko, stare at the two men, now eye to eye. Isaiah spits on the ground in front of Juan.

"You have come to terrorize anyone who doesn't conform to your idea of what it means to be Spanish. But, I tell you, we are Spanish too."

Juan steps forward and slaps the man hard across the right side of his face with his gloves. It takes a moment to recover, but Isaiah promptly lunges at Juan, trying to take him to the ground, but the soldiers are on him in a flash of silver and sword. Isaiah's wife begins to scream and tries to stop the soldiers, but she's smacked and carted away to the alley by the beastly soldier.

Marko silently rushes to grab Laura, instinctively protecting her.

She clings to Marko and whispers vehemently, "What are we going to do?!"

"We can't stay here."

"But that man! And the woman?"

Marko shakes Laura's shoulders softly but with a firm hold, "Aishe! We are gypsies to them, not Romani, you understand? We *cannot* get involved. The Inquisition is real."

Chilling screams come from the alley. In front of the building, Isaiah now lies unconscious, soaked in blood. The crowd begins to panic. The soldiers have a taste for blood and go looking for more as they walk into the crowd, looking everyone over. People point and yell at each other, and the crowd scrambles in every direction, seeking safety from the inquisitors.

One large fat man runs away, pointing at Laura and Marko, "Gypsies over here! Nasty *zíngaros*!" Just a moment before he had been enjoying the dancing with the rest of the villagers and now he turns to save his skin by getting the soldiers' attention. Juan turns his full attention onto Laura and Marko. Marko puts his body in front of Laura, who's already shaking with terror.

Marko points in another direction to distract them for a second and pushes Laura, "Run!" Marko quickly takes off the other way. The chaotic crowd gives enough coverage for Aishe to escape.

Villagers run quickly in both directions past the barrel, behind which Laura hides and tries to catch her breath. She's shaking violently, uncertain if what she's just experienced was real; it was such a bizarre turn of events. One moment she's in love, dancing with her partner in a passionate and lively performance, and the next she's hiding like a hunted animal in the street. Screams still come from the village square, and Laura sees a soldier beating up a man in the alley not far from her hiding place. With a start, Laura scootches back too far and knocks the barrel over. The noise grabs the soldier's attention.

"Stop right there!" But Laura stumbles out and runs down the alley to make for the church. The guard kicks the man one last time and starts after Laura.

Banging on the church doors, Laura screams for her life to Brother Guillermo to let her in.

"Help me! Please!" The doors open wide and the monk stands before Laura; a look of shock covers his face. He looks around and ushers Laura into the church.

"Come in, my child!" Laura grabs the monk's arm and follows him inside.

"Brother, the village square—" The monk pats her arm.

"I know." He nods his head in genuine concern. "This is an uncertain time for many."

Laura looks up at the monk, with wide eyes. "We have to do something."

"We cannot interfere, Aishe. Those men are doing God's work."

Once the words sink in, Laura abruptly steps back from the monk. "How can you say that?"

The monk folds his hands in front of him, suddenly appearing complicit. "My dear, it is God's purpose that we all be pure of faith and blood. Even the gypsies."

Laura, shocked at the monk's sudden turn of allegiance, raises her eyebrows, but an afterthought lets her realize that, of course, he would be on their side, on "God's" side, that is. Whatever the Divine Right of the King decides is God's word… "So the decrees, they are serious?"

"Yes! What is happening outside these walls will inevitably happen to you and your family, if you do not conform."

Laura gasps and, weak from fear, falls slowly to her knees.

"There is a way to protect yourself and your family."

Laura looks up hopefully at the monk. "Anything."

"You must renounce your gypsy ways. Find honorable employment, settle down, and give up the devil's dance."

Laura can't believe she's been so naïve, that she's only recently seeing the reality of the Inquisition. She begins to cry, and her tears fall heavily on the stone slabs of the church floor.

She begins to mutter to herself through her tears, "But, it is who we are. It is… it is who I am."

Brother Guillermo lays his hand on Laura's head. "But my child, it is the only way to ensure your safety."

"If I make this choice, the Church will protect us, right?"

Nodding his head yes, the monk takes Laura's hand and helps her up. Laura continues to cry and agrees to her fate.

Luca sits and plays his Spanish guitar. Gillie, next to him, enjoys the music as she mends one of Laura's skirts.

The door bursts open and Laura stumbles into the wagon. "Mama? Papa! Oh Papa." Luca and Gillie stop short and rush to Laura, thinking something terrible has happened.

"What is it? My little swan, you're crying?"

Laura flings herself into Lucas' arms. "Ai, Papa! It was horrible. The blood... the blood that spilled." Laura begins to sob. Luca wraps his arms around Laura and gives Gillie a quizzical glance, "Now, now. Shh…"

Laura desperately explains, "They came after us."

Luca pats Laura's hair. Gillie grabs Laura's hands and kisses them.

"Just because we are Romani? You know they call us 'gypsies'?"

The look of understanding now crosses her parents' faces, the same old story… "Sweet little swan, you're safe now."

Surprised by his daughter, Luca lets her go as she pushes herself out of his arms. She starts breathing hard and she shakes her head. "No, we are not! Brother Guillermo said we must follow the mandates, and then he and the Church will protect us.

Luca grunts. "*Boja*. We will never deny who we are, just for the sake of safety, Aishe. I would rather die than turn my back on my people."

Laura claws at Luca's shirt. She looks like a wild animal. "But, Papa! I don't want to die. I want to live, and if that means following—"

Luca grabs Laura's shoulders and gives her a shake. "Calm down, child!"

"No! We have to leave!" she screams, shaking her head wildly.

Luca smacks Laura across the face. "No child of mine will talk like that. We will not leave."

Laura, now snapped out of her hysteria, touches her face where her father, her supposed protector, has left a bruise. She begins to sob and rushes out of the wagon and right into Marko's arms. He grabs Laura and embraces her in a hug.

"Oh, thank God, you're safe."

As he lets her go, Laura notices Marko's lip is bloody. "Oh, Marko." She touches his face gently. "It was horrible." Laura buries her head in his shoulder. "I was so scared."

"Me too! I'm so glad you're safe."

Laura looks up at him and speaks to his eyes, "I ran to the church, and the monk said that if we follow the mandates, the Church will protect us."

Marko, confused by his betrothed's words, slowly releases himself from her embrace and puts his hands on her shoulders, looking into her eyes for clarification. "What are you talking about?"

"If we leave the camp and settle down, we'll be safe from this madness, Marko!"

He holds her shoulders steady, now with her

parents listening in and agreeing with their young daughter's husband to be.

Marko explains the reality in only a few words. "We cannot leave. This is our life. Please don't ever say those words again."

"But we won't have a life to live if we stay."

Marko hugs Laura in a long close embrace. "I will keep us safe."

But Laura pushes away from him, searching his eyes for some sanity. "No, you won't; you can't! Today is proof of that!"

Laura runs off toward the stream, in disbelief and heavy grief that her family, and especially her love, Marko, cannot see that their only way out is to simply do as the mandates decree; such a simple gesture for peace. But her allegiance to *la família* is strong.

How could I even be contemplating this? She paces back and forth by the slow rush of water on this now gentle night, slowly calming herself from the day's terrorizing events. *I love being a Romani. But, our lives are in danger. Shouldn't we choose life? Why can't they see that?* She sits down in front of a large rock and rests her back on its cool face, staring out at the stream and the knowing waters rushing by. *I don't want to die.*

A piercing bang resounds from behind the tree line. Laura stands up and faces the trees, now appearing as sentinels between her and her people. Screams come from the camp and Laura immediately runs toward her home and family only to find Marko in a pool of blood, next to the wagon. She lunges toward him and crashes to her knees next to his still warm body. She shakes him, but he doesn't move. In a panic Laura stands and looks around, her eyes wild and full of tears. She begins to search the camp.

"Agh! Mama? Papa?" She watches as soldiers beat her people. Some women are swung over the soldiers' shoulders and shoved into wagons. Finally, Laura sees Luca from across the camp.

"Papaaaa! Aieee!" she screams. Luca glances over his shoulder at his beloved daughter. So young, he sees her for the last time. He mouths words to her but they are incomplete and unintelligible. Laura stops in her fearful tracks, as the conquistador smacks Luca down with a lance, his head barely attached to his body as he hits the ground.

In a rage, Laura screams, "Naaooooooo! Papa!" The soldier has a new target and swings his lance at Laura, but she runs like the wind, passing burning wagons and many bodies, everything seemingly on fire.

Laura finds her way through the fields and runs through the village. She bangs on the church door. "*Santuario!* Sanctuary—*Padre*! The monk opens the door. Behind him stands Juan Valdos and a few of the men from the village square.

"Aishe!" The monk privately wishes she hadn't come to him, but he knows he must try to convince the conquistadors of her sincerity to convert.

"What's this, a gypsy *puta*?" The soldier wastes no time to grab Laura's arm. She yanks her arm away, but the soldier then quickly grabs both arms and holds them behind Laura's back.

The monk turns to Juan. "Your Magistrate, this girl has come to me seeking sanctuary and redemption. She is committed to leaving her Romani ways."

Laura tries to free herself, for which the soldier promptly retaliates by breaking both her wrists with one brutally powerful snap of a move. Her scream fills the anteroom, just as a weapon itself, and she almost passes out from the searing pain.

Juan stares at the soldier, who reports, "We found her in the gypsy camp."

Juan sneers at Laura and turns to the monk to say with full contempt, "The law has already been broken. You can't change these filthy swine."

"But, she has called for sanctuary."

Juan takes the heavenly padre to the church door and slams it on his hand. Laura closes her eyes at this, and resolves to a stream of tears and cries.

"Sanctuary is a right reserved only for purebloods. You may pray for her soul, but her fate is sealed. Take her away."

With her remaining strength, Laura squirms and fights against her captor, "No! NO! Brother Guillermo, *help* me!"

Juan lets the monk's hand drop, and the sweet man crosses himself with his prayer beads, holding his hurt arm close to his chest.

Laura feels as if time has moved to slow motion. She hears herself scream in the distance, a muffled terror springing from her mouth. She fights to release the soldier's grip on her. A faraway voice fades in.

"In a few moments, when I count from one to ten, go to the very end of that lifetime, to the very last moments, but with no pain, no discomfort, just to remember how you left that time, that place; just float above that scene, above that body, to connect to you now in your current life. What are the connections? You float in this beautiful space and now you feel free and light; you've left that body, that time and place… so free, so peaceful, so light… for you, is there any knowledge, wisdom or understanding to help you to remove blocks and obstacles to your inner peace and joy?

"Soon it will be time to return to full waking consciousness but you'll remember everything that you experienced. So saying goodbye to your spiritual friends and others in the time and space you're in; now rejoining your body in the beach garden, your body filled with the light has been healing… now feeling yourself back in your body, back in this room, completely grounded in your body.

"I will bring you back to full waking consciousness in complete control of body and mind. You'll be awake and alert when I count up from one to ten, and, with each number, you'll be more and more alert. By ten completely awakened, alert, and in full control of your body and mind: ONE feeling great filled with this beautiful soft energy remembering everything that you just experienced all the way back; TWO, THREE, gently awakening now; FOUR, FIVE, SIX, more and more awakened, alert, feeling great, feeling wonderful; SEVEN, EIGHT, NINE, TEN. Good. Let your eyes open and stretch if you feel like it and come all the way back; we'll stop the music and come all the way back, back to full waking consciousness."

But Laura was stuck in 1592 Catalan. Dr. McTavish's voice mutes next to the intensity of her life-or-death escape. The soldier loses his grasp of Laura and hits the ground with a grunt; her survival instinct immediate and dynamic, she lunges forward with a scream, manages to stand, and tries to run. With brute force and the speed of a trained officer, the soldier moves like a sharp northern wind, lifts his cutlass, and slices deep into Laura's hips from behind. Everything fades black.

"Laura? Laura…" Dr. McTavish firmly held Laura's arm as she resisted the return.

Laura bolted upright in the chair. She gasped for air. Her hands braced the sides of the chair. Laura looked around. Dr. McTavish moved to Laura's side. She grabbed his shirt.

"Laura, are you all right?"

"I, I have to go back. Send me back!"

Dr. McTavish grabbed Laura's hand and soothed for some time until her breathing calmed and she realized where she was, now fully back to the present 2019 Brooklyn. "Laura, the mind is unlikely to revisit this memory again."

"But you don't understand! I have to go back!"

Dr. McTavish's assistant retrieved the wheelchair. A tear rolled down Laura's face. "My dear, we've looked back, now's the time to start looking forward."

Laura hung her head low.

"I made a terrible choice and… it didn't change anything."

"Exploring memories can be traumatizing, but you have to learn from them. That's part of the journey."

Laura looked up at Dr. McTavish. She calmed down. "I have to know more!"

"There are more journeys to be taken; if you're willing… Today was a wonderful start."

Laura looked up at Dr. McTavish with wide eyes. "There are more?"

GLOSSARY

assoluta	Italian word for "absolute" (e.g., prima ballerina *assoluta* – lead ballerina)
Baile	Catalan for "dance!"
Bo	Catalan for "good"
Boja	Catalan for "crazy"
Buenos matin	Spanish/Catalan for "good morning"
Chiquita	Spanish/Catalan for "little girl"
čurák	Czech vulgarity for an extremely unpleasant man (dick)
el meu elegante cisne	Catalan for "my elegant swan"
el meu nen	Catalan for "my child"
escudos	Spanish gold, bronze, or silver coins, used as currency at the time
gallinas	Spanish/Catalan for "hens"
gitanos	the Romani people in Spain, belonging to the Iberian Kale ethnic group
golpe	Catalan for "percussive tapping" used with flamenco

	guitar and body rhythms
hijo	Catalan for "son"
kabanosy	dry, thinly sliced Polish sausage
kanapki	common Polish breakfast sandwich
Mako shark	the mako is the fastest shark on Earth
meu amor	Catalan for "my love"
Milonguera	avid tango dancer (female)
nens	Catalan for "children"
Ole	common Spanish/Catalan exclamation similar to "yay!"
palmas	Catalan for "palms"
soumak	Caucuses tapestry technique of weaving strong and decorative textiles used as rugs and domestic bags
tilaka	Sanskrit for a colorful mark, worn usually on the forehead
tu puta	Spanish/Catalan for "you whore"
Zigeunerin	German for "Romani"
zíngaros	derogatory Spanish/Catalan term for the Romani people, much like "gypsy"

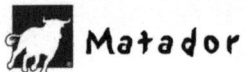

For exclusive discounts on Matador titles,
sign up to our occasional newsletter at
troubador.co.uk/bookshop